DRAIN SONGS

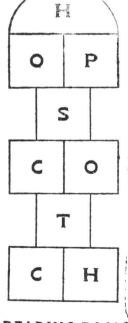

DRAIN SONGS

GRANT MAIERHOFER

STORIES AND A NOVELLA

TUSCALOOSA

Copyright © 2019 by Grant Maierhofer
The University of Alabama Press
Tuscaloosa, Alabama 35487-0380
All rights reserved

FC2 is an imprint of The University of Alabama Press

Inquiries about reproducing material from this work should be addressed to the University of Alabama Press

Book Design: Publications Unit, Department of English, Illinois State University; Director: Steve Halle, Production Assistants: Hope Rutgens
Cover image: <TK, if needed>
Cover Design: Lou Robinson
Typeface:

Earlier versions of these stories have appeared in *The Fanzine*, *NY Tyrant*, *X-Ray Lit*, *Egress*, *Numero Cinq*, and the *Writers in the Attic* Song issue. The author is grateful in turn to these publications and the Department of English at the University of Idaho.

Library of Congress Cataloging-in-Publication Data is available from the Library of Congress.

ISBN: 978-1-57366-074-7

E-ISBN: 978-1-57366-885-9

This book is dedicated to the memory of my father,
William James Maierhofer,
I love you and miss you more every day

For Kelsey, Ada, Hollis, and Elisabeth

CONTENTS

1   Lifers
15 Maintenance Art
25 Bruxism
37 Boredoms
43 Everybody's Darling
55 Drain Songs

"Our home is a closed space, closed to the weather and to the sound and fury of the practical and productive world. Windows open our retreat, our lair, to the world, but view the weather from behind glass and view the hubbub and fury of the street and the city from above. Our window is separated from the smooth and striated space of the street and the city by the smoothest of smooth spaces: the empty air. Death by leaping from a window is different from death by inducing, through drugs, a final withdrawal in the quiet retreat of a home."

—"Defenestration," Alphonso Lingis

DRAIN SONGS

LIFERS

My name is Lyle. I'll leave it at that so far as ID. I'll go on however to say that, if you're feeling generous, I may contain multitudes. I'd like to think this way. I'd like to silence the doubt of me and scream it out in gold handsful. I may be dense with potential. I may desire the entire world. I'm a failure in so many words. I'm tired of feeling this way and so I'm trying to contain those words myself, to write them out. I want my feelings to be expressed so I might move on from them. I should like to be rid of me. I want to put some distance between myself and this place wherein I find myself. Other night I went to the gas station only to find lips and eyes still caked with black makeup. I keep a feather from my mother's boa tucked against my breast. I might sing to myself in the mirror until I'm bored. I live in sorrow. My days are full of thorns, people and bosses. I tend toward the sad, the weary. I'm an avid person though, romantic even. I want to contain the world. I am a male but I would like a womb to contain the world. I'd like for my eyes always to be smeary with experiment and mascara. I should be so lucky.

I think I've slept for most of my days. I don't mean it literally. I mean the stupor. I mean that as I graduated high school, as I saw my youth pass, I had these glazed eyes and didn't care to open them beyond mere ability to see. Sometimes this can happen. Sometimes people aren't meant to express themselves in any recognizable way, any acceptable way. My father was, by and large, this way. He had crazed tendencies, I gather. He'd left the house under certain pretenses, returned under others. He was always shifting shapes, nobody but my mother tried to keep up. I think this is what happened, anyway. I was sleeping. In retrospect I pass no judgment on the pair. We are the lot of us a working class, and each of us ought to be allowed our nightly ruts.

    I spent a long time needing to escape, and found it in the beds of lonely old men and women. From each I'd keep a souvenir and affix it to the inside of my leathers. There was always quiet after in their bathrooms where I'd pray. I'd torture myself in slight degrees with ever-tightening metal barbs. Lately I've returned. I work now at the high school where I used to hide away. When you're young everybody's terrible. When you grow up everything's terrible. Something changes between these in that things get worse, darker. Mostly, however, they are the same.

Each day I put on gray coveralls that you have seen. I push a cart that was given to me by an old man. This old man, my predecessor, had lost his wife. His kids were away, succeeding. This old man had lived a full life before this work. Then, losing his wife, his children, he found himself wanting. This old man sought work and found the position he'd occupied for seven years before I took it on. He trained me for a few weeks and then supervised, then left entirely. I think he might be dead.

    The cart holds a garbage can that I'll fill three or four times each day, depending. Kitchen staff attend to their cans and I'm grateful for it. Some days, events or come what may, I might focus primarily on trash. The school isn't large. It would take an event or more to fill my can beyond three or four times each day, I'm saying. I remember when I was younger, going here, and we'd attempt to fill the can from distances with paper cartridges of milk. These were shaped like ships or small homes. We called them cartridges, and lofted them into the janitor's can as he'd walk by. Looking back he'd never register this, even once maintaining composure when my cartridge of chocolate milk pelted his chest and landed. I'm now more understanding of his intimacy with death and suffering.

So anyway, I don't live in my father's basement. So anyway, I've got my own place. I'm fairly certain the person who lived here previous was a criminal, a felon. He left quickly and so far as I can tell the rent plummeted. My neighbors pay dearly. I pay a pittance because some crook likely opened his scalp where I eat my dinners. Give and take, sure. I spend my days when not working walking around this area. I like to grab a pizza, maybe, or Chinese, and sit with it staring off. I'd like to say I appear as some kind of threat. I hate this town, is all. I don't think that's what happens, though. Sometimes people recognize me and laugh. The worst is the high school kids. They'll get pizza themselves, sure. Chinese, whatever. They'll be out to eat and talking, talking and building their lives together. They'll look over and see me, it's often tough to stomach.

Then, after this, then, I'll often try to make for the city. You understand, I hope. This town where I work is small but aware enough. They talk, you see. They'll talk, each and all of them. I'm not a fan of talkers. I'm a fan of light. So what do I do?

In my room I go to the closet. There I've hung them, and others. Most nights I've got these leather pants, sure. I've got my T-shirts. I've got my boots, they shine a bit. I'll put these on and sort of air my hair a bit. Somewhere when I was younger I loved KISS. Now they're just O.K., mostly morons. I think maybe that's where it started, though. So I'll put on black lipstick. I'll put on eye makeup and smear it down. I'll light some Salems and put on my music. I'll put on Pentagram. I'll put on Venom. I'll put on Saint Vitus and sort of air out. I'm tall, you see. My outfit's black. My pants are leather. Living when I live, then, it can be tough to feel free. So where to go? I've found some places. I like the leather bars on karaoke nights. Mostly people there will want a pickup. It's fine, sure. I've made with men and women. I've dated a bit. I don't go for this, though. I like the sounds. I like to feel a speaker press my body. Sometimes a burlesque, maybe, but often I'll worry about teachers on a whim. Bored depressives with obvious hard-ons. Have at it, I mean. I'm O.K. with all types. I just want noise.

My favorite kind of night blurs the whole thing. These

barflies from the '70s and '80s had taken it upon themselves to give strange metal bands and such their due. Having no patience, however, for meatheads and fascism, they catered to groups of outsiders who'd play pool and dance, drink and come together, take drugs or write their names on walls. Some performance endeavor rumored to have been Prince's fallback had his tenure at First Avenue proved too tame, and these bodies took it upon themselves to keep his assless chapseat warm. Good citizens, all.

I'd like to state, however, a pressing thing: it took me fucking *years* to find my way. Where I worked, forget it. You find all sorts of lonely gentlemen after handjobs in parking lots. I partook. I'm grateful I partook as I was lonely too, but something always missed. I sat in audiences at drag shows and queer karaoke nights in otherwise square bars with no sense of welcome. I wore out my eyes on the internet until having eventually to masturbate myself to sleep. It took me fucking years.

I used to read a lot about New York and wanted to go there, before AIDS and before David Wojnarowicz had to sew his lips shut and before the murder and definition and language seeped through everything. I wanted bodies in rooms and their voices muffled against what. A shoulder or bathroom divider. It was my way home of seeking peace I think. I was always performing. I don't know that this is a bad way to live. We have jobs, right? We have accounts and ways of being sought and keys to apartments and homes. We have children and responsibilities and worlds. I feel that we earn performance through this, even brief stints of fucking in cars, bodies blurring. The more I worked the more I drenched myself in black. The more I lived the more I became the fiction.

One day in question I had found myself hiding frequently at work. This happened often. I became tired of the same faces staring at me as I pulled their stuffed plastic bottles of trash from drinking fountains and whatever else. I'd clean the bathrooms thoroughly then. I'd work my way from floor to ceiling with bleach and whatever materials I had in decent supply as all of this was arguably necessary. Students were superficially disgusting. Teenagers were superficially disgusting. They'd cake layers of themselves onto the tiles and this could be a chore to get removed. What I was doing didn't matter, but looked appropriate enough. I had let life reach me and get to me and all I wanted to do was curl up someplace institutional and weep. I'd been to hospitals. I'd been a dum dum boy. The tears would well. I couldn't weep, though, so I did as I've suggested. I put things off as long as I could to get my work done. I smiled at my boss and I made sure every bathroom looked excessively clean and jotted somewhere that I'd done something of necessity.

At night, however, I might be free. I went to the gas station near me on walking home and purchased a tall can of cheap booze. I don't often drink before arriving in the city but I was feeling rotten. On arriving home I removed all of my clothes from work. I paced around my living room smoking and cursing the day before opening my booze. My bathroom is small and dimly lit. My body looks alright in dim light, I think. I looked at myself. I pulled my hair back and made lips at myself there in the dingy mirror. I ran my hands up the sides of my frame and felt my ribs, warmed a bit with pleasure or sex. I put liner on my eyes and smeared it down, kissing the mirror and leaving the day's worker grease. I put black lipstick on and stood briefly on the tub's ledge staring, then pulling on my leathers and a too-small shirt from when I played baseball as a boy. The shirt rose up just above my navel and as I hunched over to pull on boots I felt it stick first then rise above my spine, my lower back. The feeling of worn fabric against me that smelled like smoke and perfume was enlivening. I wanted more.

I think about stories I could tell. My father could tell stories, could lie. I wonder about this. What creates a tendency toward fabrication? Is my split a fabrication? Would I be better off in therapy than writing out my thoughts? Where do I start and end if my need for writing is purely selfish? I have nothing to say and I'm not even whispering it. I do not have answers, but in the car I listened to Whitney Houston. I find what I think of as her transmitted vulnerability empowering. I'll often sit and listen to her in the bath and hold my chest. When she died my sister called me concerned. I was sitting in the bathtub with the lights out humming to myself. I'll occasionally obsess over this sort of voice. I left town and drove to the city amid lights and drank at my can of booze. I'd ease my arm out the window and let it sway there on the wind. I'd smoke with the other as the can cooled my crotch. I felt feral. I felt set free. I felt my body boiling up with all the misery of my days and the stares of the students and I ran it out my hair, stared at myself in the sun-down mirror and the running makeup, performing.

I wanted to quiet my head further so on arrival I drank several vodka tonics and sat sneering from the bar. I felt the booze warm my gut and my mood began to lift, yipping maybe toward a nice oblivion as the room filled up with barely-clothed bodies kissing and sucking at each other. Men running hands over one another or women twirling hair to rhythms. Everyone reaching some fluidity and pushing to the edges of abjection on leather and neon fabrics only to be pulled back. I sat and watched until the pulse of it warmed me over.

I went into the bathroom after writhing against some fleshy bits and denim and found two gentlemen coupling. They were taller, like myself, so it wasn't trying to see them in the stall pressed to the wall and howling. The music in there was slightly quieter and thus I heard their groans as I stared into the mirror and ran the sink to wet my hands. Eventually I noticed someone crouched in the corner of the space and turned to see.

I haven't made a point of meeting many people where I work. I don't care for them nor they I. This is as it is. I am O.K. under these circumstances. This person I'd seen perhaps helping around the office, perhaps guiding buses toward the end of day. I can't and couldn't recall, but I knew her and knew her from work. I walked to her and registered a horror peeling the skin of her face back at being alive. Her eyes bugged out. The swelter of the room became heavy and miserable then. The gentlemen the stall over persisted in their fucking. She looked at me and didn't seem to register a likeness, a sufferer with which to commune. I went to the sink for water and wetted a paper towel, returning and pressing it to her forehead. Her skin was pale. She was sweating incessantly. She smelled medical. I tried to touch my hand to her cheek to check the temperature there, encourage some level of identification. She grabbed my wrist and began pulling me toward her. I stood and she came with me. We stood together and she seemed barely to note the gentlemen in the stall near us. I don't know or care much for drugs. I drink and have partaken, little more. This was something horrific. This was all the world pressing at my chest. I felt my fingers. They were dried up. They were shriveled. I couldn't make sense of it. I'd run them under water awhile. I'd been sweating. I felt my chest heave and wanted to collapse.

The girl wanted to leave. I could see it. She wouldn't vocalize. She grabbed my wrist again. We walked together through the black and swelter, the light and drink, until the cold night air shocked something into us. I felt myself coming together. I felt myself falling apart. I vomited there, or somewhere, walking toward the parking lot. I vomited and it hit the knee of my leathers and I only know it in retrospect. She pulled my wrist. Next day, maybe, I noticed redness there. She was quiet. Her hair was short, brown but slicked in spots against her skull. Her shirt was white and not ripped but mangled against her chest, small gut and arms. She wore a coat and dressed in pants and shoes as if she'd only just left the school to come here. Her hands were shriveled and I felt them abrade my wrist and slither. I wore my barbs high up on the right arm and they caught briefly at the back of her coat. I suppose she had a car as mine was only caked with my debris.

I don't remember coherent things then. I remember laying

back or being fully prone on her backseat, our legs however they needed to be to mash us there. I remember staring up at the back window and feeling calm through its fog, its slightly frozen coat and her hands against my ribs. I do not think that she and I in fact fucked. Both of her cold hands, though, these pressed against the sides of me and held me there and she made no recognizable sounds. She made groans, sure. She perhaps whispered things against me and sweated through her clothes and mine, imploring me to stay until the light. I felt the sickness of bile at the back of my throat and through to the next day. I can still feel the cold of her seat against my head. I remember knowing something. I remember the sounds of those gentlemen and wishing life could be that simple. I recognized her and felt pulled to her. I don't know what my sense of responsibility was that night. I might've called 911, though I found no evidence the next day. We might've fucked, sure. I have experienced memory loss. I have missed days of my life staring off, asleep, not caring. I can piece together fragments only. Fragments of her wrists, say. Fragments of her hair and its slickness against my cheek, my mouth. The whispering and grunting at my chest, the howling even. These are my memories. This was an anomalous moment, a night that doesn't fit. I found myself in complete lack of control and things seemed to spiral out in front of me. Perhaps she wanted to die. Perhaps she'd found that room to hear people fucking nearby so she might die near them. This makes sense to me. I can appreciate this impulse. Perhaps someone drugged her and she barely escaped. I trust the people there but I have a male body and there are differences, bars and clubs vary in degree of insidiousness or threat, perhaps. I'm uncertain how to piece anything together in retrospect. I only remember the window. I only remember the gloss of night and the armor of our coats around us as we held there against whatever death.

 I woke with her stomach's skin against mine, cold but for the small strip where we touched. I worried she was dead, then my head felt like it was being crushed beneath the sea, then a drunken bubble rose and I smelled vomit. I must have spoken with her but all I remember is her mumbling. I must have sat up and tried to figure things out but all that stands out are the lights on driving home. I think I spoke to her. I think I sat her up and made sure she could function well enough. I would've looked for something to straighten her out, a bottle of water maybe or a bit of food. I would've tried to do these things. I'm not sure which things I did and didn't do. I hoped that I did everything. I woke later and still hoped that I did everything.

 I don't know how to advocate or speak for another. I couldn't have made her situation better or worse. She looked like me: her hair was matted in memory, her clothing a messy sprawl of unkempt materials, I remember all of it looking like escape, the both of us seemingly wanting to flee. I don't remember what we said or whether we touched more on waking. I don't remember if she was O.K. that night or what. I don't remember feeling any relief or vomiting in my walk to my car. I only remember the lights as I began to surface driving across a bridge to my town. I remember sitting at a McDonald's terribly early and drinking cup after cup of water and coffee, slowly putting myself back together only long enough to return to my small home and fall asleep caked in sweat and ugly smells until the afternoon.

Later on that week when I saw her outside of school as I walked my can toward the large dumpster I felt nauseous. I doubt if she recognized me. When I woke up from that night and looked in the mirror I might've been any anonymous body soaked in strobe and the mud of people. It didn't matter if she recognized me. I walked by and felt my anonymity. I felt myself return to my youth in that hell and was calm and glazed over by the notion; asleep and it started at the eyes. Bells rang and children abounded. Groups assembled themselves at the doors of classrooms wherein they'd make minor messes throughout the afternoon. That evening two shows were being put on and I was asked to keep things orderly afterward. I'd accepted gratefully as things had felt amiss since waking in that car. I was always fairly close to death, I figure. I had never seen someone OD and this was something to process, maybe. I was feeling my whole world curl in on itself and become ruinous. I tended to ruin. I was a ruiner. I moved the can across the sidewalk having left a numbered door and made my way past the lot of them leaving to lives filled with people. That night I might dress myself or lie on the floor naked to feel my limbs sprawl out. That night I might open the windows and let in the cold to touch my skin. That night I might drink myself stupid and feel aligned with planets. I wasn't sure. I walked by and felt the identifying touch of stomach as I passed her. Everything seemed O.K. Everything would be O.K. for me in turn. This has always been my problem. These have always been my problems. I am always gnashing my teeth against the low guts of life only to rise again to my mediocrity. I await the weekend when I'll perform.

MAINTENANCE ART

When she wakes her feet stick and scrape against the sheet. He is gone, has gone for the day. The bed and the room were larger, she spread herself out in yawning. The winter dried out her feet, created rifts of skin that lagged on carpets and made sleep a nuisance, waking this way. She felt pain, misery at finding herself that way. The room had too much light and the gray surrounding her was nauseating. The gown she wore, to the knee, had twisted around her and as she rose it conflicted with her and pulled her back to be. She sat facing the wall, gathering breath, bedside table on the right. She opened her pills, took them. She had a bit of water from the night before and drank before standing up. She stood and drove her fist slowly into the wall, pushing but getting nowhere.

The night had made her sweat, she was chilled. She stood staring at his side of the bed scratching herself and making faces. They had no children, a cat. They were aging together.

He was a bit moronic, a loudmouth. They'd met and drowned one another out and this had worked. He could be kind, open. On most days this was welcome.

She walked into the bathroom and stared at the mirror. She pulled up her hand near her face and waited. She slapped herself three times and continued to stare, the skin there reddening and a warmth of pain spreading then. She spit at the mirror and screamed out. This was an unhappy ordeal. She was an unhappy presence to stare at. Always this fixation with the skin.

Somehow, what happened, she began to smirk. He could be so trying. He could be so empty-headed, staring there. She laughed aloud and gripped the sink handles taut, squeezing a moment and letting it pass, then gesturing in opposite directions, X-ing her body, pulling inward as the sink turned on. Awkwardly, she put her face beneath the nozzle and let the lukewarm water spread over her temple. Nights and days this way just made her crazy.

***

Showered, she pulled on jeans and T-shirt, shirking bra et cetera in favor of simple, workaday fabrics. Downstairs she petted the cat as it wended its way in figure-eight against her calves and shins, pulled on light tennis shoes and made for the car. This was a cumbersome day in a cumbersome year made of talking and television. Nights they'd do this. Nights they'd fuck and wash at fluids after. Nights he'd read of crime or something and she might lay perfectly still, scrolling through her phone and looking through the lives of friends and former lovers as she imagined their thumbs, jerkily playing over light and doing same. Nights she'd stand outside and pull at flecks of skin that wouldn't sit right, just be fed on blood or oxygen or light but she would itch.

Phantom pains or esoteric descriptors of her state or its symptoms did not interest her much. Therapy had run its course thus. Talking had become exhausting almost immediately. Recounting a life in rooms had proven mere distraction.

Leaving a marriage was fine. He had left a marriage. She didn't want to enact clichés. She wanted to shift the locus of her days. A home is problematic. Leaving a marriage was impossible. She didn't want to leave.

This was how people lived. She saw them. Driving she saw men and women and men and men and women and women and iterations of each in numerous hues unloading kids, pets, suitcases, purses, tents, paperwork, lunches, coats, all of these from cars parked in driveways like her own outside of schools like ones nearby, everything this slew of searching meat and plastic, cotton and rubber staving off a godly heave. She farted in the car and turned on music. She did smile. She unrolled her window and smelled the cold. She drove downtown to the university where she worked. She pulled a bag from her backseat on parking and lugged it into a tall brick building, very old.

***

On her shelves within her office were various works and images. Names of people in large part from Europe lined the spines of books and images were mostly from a simpler time wherein she didn't dwell. Now she dwelled, unbuttoned her jeans and set her feet atop her desk, pulling a thin blanket her mother had sent her years ago from Greece. The blanket was purple and let light show through, still subtly blurring pure sight. Behind her desk the window halved the brick and where she sat was quaint. She was quaint. She detested what quaintness she perceived in herself. She stared at the books by the French and tried to feel alive. She read of Louis Althusser murdering his wife and became terrified. The domestic had its way of bleeding over into primitive hell. The mind had its tendency of crowding out all speech. The potential of anything so extreme within her closed her mind.

***

A student came in to discuss the work at hand.

"Well, I, uhh, is it there?" she felt a nod within, twiddled a bit at the button of her jeans and faced the student, a bulky male of athletic stature, ability.

"I want to talk to you about this work." *I want, to be sure, to scrape my teeth over the screen of this computer, to see your future astride titan backs of sporting gooders when I wake from this nightmare.*

"And so, we will . . . What I tried to do here was merge the sense, uhh . . . This thing you talked about in class . . . To merge the concerns of the Frenchman, uhh . . . "

"Frenchman, yes, sure . . . "

"With bodies? To merge this with how, erm . . . With how I see my friends engaging with . . . The internet . . . "

"Correct. This is apparent, I assure you. I see this in your writing. I see you merging, and it is apt. To your former point, the *there*ness? It might never, *never*, be up to me." *What I envy, in my pittance that I've gathered here, the dust in front of my shoes which I've chosen to deem my stake, my life, what I'm due, what I envy are things* *like bleach. I envy the force of bleach. The desire of bleach. The ease with which it does what's needed and drains itself, removing all traces beyond olfactory that it took up your space, your time.*

"Yea uhh, well yea, definitely. I just, uhh, I wanted to be sure I wasn't veering off, right? I feel myself veer off when writing. I try to sit and think, whatever . . . It just doesn't happen so easy for me . . . "

"I would assure you, here, of your aptness. I would assure you of my confidence. I enjoy to see this work, this *veering*. Any we've read, their quests—to my mind—were not for certainty. Others will tell you otherwise, as is their wont. My wont is no such thing. I trust you. I want to see where the work takes you."
I want to fall apart, openly. I want to be screaming and dragged off, my entire unease made palpable and immediate. I want to be a little girl upon the family dog, commanding villages of plastic.

***

Within the university's library after her office hours were complete she sought brief respite. Within this library there were shelves of materials and students at computers and students sleeping and students arguing or masturbating or inhaling drugs and there were bathrooms. Strewn like vertebrae up the floors of the library were bathrooms that featured copious locks. She had taken in recent months to setting up a sort of second set of office hours therein, where real work was done. There, she opened a rented copy of *Culture and Value* and read of all the inevitable failures of all the spaces she occupied.

"If you have a room which you do not want certain people to get into, put a lock on it for which they do not have the key. But there is no point in talking to them about it, unless of course you want them to admire the room from outside! The honorable thing to do is put a lock on the door which will be noticed only by those who can open it, not by the rest." *Ludwig says this and I hear him and I feel nauseated. I think of the boy who asked me simple questions. I think of simple questions, lives enacted and ordered based on this. I feel comforted. I think of Ludwig leaving the world to build a home for his sister, was it. I think of Ludwig and the church, of prayer. I think of him returning later on. I have found no means to flee.*

She reads this and other passages and blows her nose. She throws the book across the room and laughs. She empties her bag upon the floor and grabs at lipstick. She writes upon the floor ALL I WANTED WERE ALL COLLEGES TO EXIT ME then smears it. The result is a mess of red, greasy markings that won't let up. She wets some paper towels and begins to sweat over the work of pulling up her etching.

***

After this she's sitting on the toilet, variously scrolling through her phone or shitting. He calls her and his image comes up over the life she'd been mining of a professor she'd once fawned over until he'd asked in an email what she was wearing.

"Heyyy," he says, a bit jovial.

"Hello hon. How are you today?" *I wanted that professor to give me anything I might need. I wanted that professor to talk to me late over coffee and encourage me in all I hoped to do. I wanted that professor to help. Help.*

"I'm good. Slow day here. Mike asked if we'd go over for pool with him and Cyn and I said *nooo wayyy*.".

"My hero. Thank you. They're nice, but . . . "

"*People are terrible.* You don't need to tell me. These fuckers."

Aside from short blips at the sink or in the car, this was a deeply fulfilling laugh.

"You are perfect."

"What're you doing?"

"I'm in the bathroom. I hate this place."

"You take your meds today?"

"I did. I. Hate. This. Place."

"I hate this place too. Rubes abound."

"Rubes?"

"My father said it. Never say it anymore. All the same, these rubes, they abound. I'm telling you."

"I've got class soon. I need to wrap things up in here."

"Sounds good. I'll grab us something on my way home. I know you hate the place. I'm sorry for it. I know things haven't been on our side. I know I ruined things last night. I promise we'll figure it out though. I promise."

"I know, hon. I'm not worried. Still. Hate. This. Place."

"I love you sweetheart. I'll see you in a few hours."

Perhaps she hadn't given him the key. Perhaps she hadn't even locked the room. Perhaps she'd told the wrong people where it was and now would suffer for it.

***

Class that afternoon was an assemblage of various media, geared toward engaged consumption and resultant conversation with these faces.

"Today, before we get working, I wanted to talk to you about a simple matter. We've discussed what faces you in generating new ideas. Novel thoughts, right? Taking the humdrum material we all have and galvanizing it into something useful for mankind." *They know that I am medicated, weeping. They see through the thick of me, the facade, my useless fucking voice. I am so tired and I just want to curl up and die. Everything is fraudulent. I am a charlatan. I am a dilettante. I have nothing new to offer anyone. I just want to leave.* "What we haven't talked about is balance. That's what I wanted to talk to you about today, then. We live unbalanced lives. Most of us anyway. We come to this to find balance only to find more and more disparity between our lived days and the minor ideas we engage with here. This is our great problem. We are living here, we are thinking too. We have to find some way to merge these things so as to avoid becoming rotten citizens." *I've only ever wanted to be a rotten citizen. My feet hurt, are scaled. My head hurts. My body rejects itself and I am losing grip. I detest the clothing, the game of purchasing and the container where I might walk off with a salad, some Diet Coke. I reject the imperative of lunch. I want pure evil. I do not want to return home tonight to my regularity. I am simple.* "Most before you have not found balance. Most choose either the life inside the head or the Norman Rockwell. I am asking you to shove your head through Norman Rockwell."

My problem is I never readied myself for the monotony of this: a day of snowy city, a husband with what, a head, some forearms maybe, eyes, the nicety of grocery stores and maintenance workers, a life in the margins in the bathroom in the brick enclosures, whatever. I've never had keys and I've never known where locks go. These slackjawed children do not care. "I talked with a student today about a Frenchman, our Frenchman, monsieur Foucault, Mr. Redolent with Death and Sex. It was brief, but I think Foucault in the street in the Night of the Barricades is what I'm getting at. Nietzsche and becoming what one is, right? Weeping over the horse maybe. Mutter, ich bin dumm. I don't want you to be students, watered down, upon your pages. I want you to let your messes through. I once worked with a teacher of mine who didn't want this. He this teacher wanted our lives in here in brick separate from whatever dullard necessities we experienced between. I think you should avoid this. I think you should seek fullness. This is my hope for you. This is where we'll start." *I am not a happy person and I'm tired of saying so. What makes someone happy. How does happiness walk, shit, get up in the morning. I would like to leave.*

***

After class she sits for an hour in her office though her husband sends her progressively more frantic texts. Her students did their work and one trailed after to discuss limit experiences. She sat at her desk with her pants unbuttoned watching videos on the internet of men confessing to crimes in court and weeping. She chewed nicotine gum and scratched avidly at her underarms. She thought of having children, didn't care. She ran her fingers under the crust of lives beneath her desk and pressed her sweating forehead to its top. This was a day, for her. These were her days.

***

At night when she can think again she's at the kitchen sink and he is sleeping. She showered after the two of them fucked shortly then argued about having a child longer. Her hair is mostly dry and the raggedy bathrobe she's had for a decade feels perfect against her, like muslin or a cold bedsheet lit by sun on waking. The sink is filling. She's tired of the sameness of her days and the domestic and the sun has gone down and the night light is bluish and it all feels subpar. Her feet still hurt and it hurts to think about her body. They'd eaten dinner and laughed and talked and things had felt relaxed. She'd worked a bit while he watched television and the cat wended itself between her calves and shins. The sink is becoming too full, the water tinged with red from something, something. She thinks of her parents as she tended to and thinks of her students and school and the professor and the work and her bitten nails and an inability to function and her feet, her medicine, the skull that held the brain being pumped with various materials and none of it seeming to work. She stares off until the sink makes noise the water dripping and she stops. She reaches her hands down into the red muck of it and feels the slimed metal and closes her eyes. The water still dripping, her feet become wet, the floor is making sounds, expanding. She runs her hands through the darkness of it until a rubber bit presents itself, small and amorphous as a heart. She holds herself there and breathes, beginning to weep into the red-tinged water. She breathes in and pulls a deep yank until the rubber makes a slurp and gives way. The noise is overwhelming as she falls to the wet ground and pulls her robe about her. The room is lit unwelcomingly. Her feet are in such pain. She stares at the entry until the cat presents itself, begins to lick a bit at the edges of the slopped red water surrounding her.

BRUXISM

"All happy families are alike, every unhappy family is unhappy in its own way,"—Leo Tolstoy

"All the things that he preaches for the happiness of humanity only complicate life to the point where it becomes harder and harder for me to live,"—Sophia Tolstaya

Come home to sister, mother, brother, asleep. They have had tiring days of late; appointmented, looming. Everyone's got glassy eyes. We line up at the bathroom about once an hour for an opportunity to quiet down. A passing took place. Abrupt, gradual, then sudden as it ripped through each of us in turn. We each needed versions of each other that were constantly eluding their follower. We circled one another never quite clicking and felt the leaving. I see the need for it and it brings about some new moods in me, and thus the nights turn. Where I've gone, my tending, is often immaterial. I shop for knives, I shop for hats. My body runs cold and I sit in the car pouring heat as I look at each weapon. I see a film; its contents haze and wander inside my cold skull as I digress within myself mourning the drive back to these empty snoring heads. Check in on them: one, two, three; there is order in the universe, peace. A balletic step from room to room, a glass of water drunk.

Nothing heavy, no loftiness or concern. We keep a cat, the cat who has its way. A family tiptoeing around a dinner table, an island in the kitchen. My mother torn up inside presses her hands against a cutting board with nothing there to cut. My sister consoles her by staring out the window in the next room. My brother protects them both from outsiders by sleeping forgetting in his bed. I keep my peace and observe the varying smells within the basement. It is an old home, on a tired street, in a small town. Purchased before children, it will likely never again exist bereft of yelling. I'm uncertain when my mother will up and decide to sell the place. Our neighbors are kind. I'm fucking weary.

"You too?" my sister asks after my mother's smoking cigarette.

"Uh-huh. Yea. Little treat."

"Nothing's funny anymore. Is Frederick going back to school?"

"Nobody's nothing. No more. Frederick might well be going back to school. Ask after him. Ask after your brother."

"Ted just sleeps. He always did. Only time without when he was going-going on those meds. Senior always said as much, 'Ted's going-going today yeah?'"

"Senior had his funny ways before the shift to nothing's funny. These've lost bite." She wetted, blended the cigarette into the porchwood, a sopping papery artwork. Through the halved basement window they looked familial, angelic. My mother the serene, my sister the energetic. I touched my hands to the concrete of the basement and felt a similar wetness to the outside damp. I rested my forehead against the cold surface and felt it wet. I turned slowly to press each temple to the concrete and stared at the curvature of room as I twisted and curled my toes firmly into the floor. I pulled my hands away so that only my head supported me and pressure began to gather there, some blood. I tried to push my head through the surface into dirt. No luck.

Frequently they'd sit there just those girls and I would listen from wherever, my carved-out places in the home. We were too linked and talkative. A room containing one contained each of our histories and my mother was always going on. It was a bit as if in his end he'd left the starts to hundreds of conversations just at the fore of our minds, each of them veering in infinite directions, never to quite connect. The home's furniture was from a previous era, flowered and all in some hue of brown regardless of its actual color. All of it comforted me. The television lined in wood, comforted me. The basement and its objects. I'd create things and mess with old machinery down there, drawing connections. I was getting on in years to live this way, some small handful of possible lives I'd already left in nearby cities. False starts, attempts, efforts. It all tended to bring me back, the series of events of late seemed cementing.

Sometimes my mother would get dressed up to watch a film on TV. I'd sit at the stool in the kitchen drinking cup after cup of coffee and my mother would be there talking to Bruce Willis about her medication. She liked the sequential weekly dose device. I'd heard it referred to more aptly by a doctor of hers once before but one night I'd imagined a conversation with my brother, us both happy, and he muttered out "sequential weekly dose device" while showering the seven days of dope across his face. Some reached his mouth, some not, we'd laughed. All a fiction. Since then I'd called it that in secret. The clouded blue plastic marked **SMTWTFS** became a sort of joke without end. The little boxes acting as the governors of her days. All connected they amounted to a week of living. Nothing warmed me like this ritual of hers. Dressing herself up just so, and sitting there with an elegant meal she'd worked over. She seemed happy then.

    Mother had her share of secrets. Without speaking directly to the matter it was an ugly series of events. The fellow gone and his pluck restored up underneath some shaven shell. He'd gone from concerned citizen to fundraising quasi-public figure to tanned cliché in the quickest series of missteps I'd seen. His new bride equally burnt but young, her own confused missteps leading her into the hair-carpeted arms and gold-watch-desperation of senior. And then there came the end, each of us bearing witness to a slightly different death and my mother out in front of it. A disease remained after in the home carrying weakness and withdrawal, my mother's, its presence seemed to hang in every doorway. His monies were eventually doled while ours dwindled. I needed work. A Country Kitchen employment opportunity. A boss a buffoon. A man I interviewed with and likened to Ted Bundy. He was always on our backs. The hearth of home reduced to sentimental hubbub. None of us bothered by it excepting in the abstract. Each a little tormented. I fell for each of my employees in their way, young and old they all seemed to tie up my loose ends. We'd serve a range of takes on slop and watery juices. The city emanated from the place of business, a diner, city hall. Just as expectant of a horde of angry villagers some nights as teenagers pressing fleshy bits of denim to their sweethearts. Good work. The boss a father figure in his head.

Sister, Ellen, had her ways of coping. An ambivalence, so to speak, such that she might find intense meanings in aisles of gas stations, experience epiphanies in friends' basements long after they'd wanted her gone. I admired that about her. Class of a different sort, economic and artful, Henry Miller she was, bereft of cock and all its superfluities. I never knew what she might be reading or getting into, which I guess explained her art. Some people have a way of being that renders the lives of the some hundred souls or so they come across as perhaps atilt, often as I'd observed it Ellen gave the push. I admired that far more for my entire misunderstanding of matters. *If I ought to be born a woman*, I might shout, *let it be in the image of Ellen.*

Even without the senior's profession mother's teeth had seen their days. I'd asked for stories on as much: she'd bitten into arms of national guardsmen on entering chained academic halls. She'd smoked ten thousand cigarettes in cars through toxic waves of desert charring the will within those teeth to yearn. She'd chewed on cups in anxiety as a girl and bit her gums to blood awaiting her father's various returns. She'd emptied more coffee in her face than Balzac and each as wired and chemical as the last. Her teeth had seen their days. She wore them almost proudly now, as aging artists might. Simply-clad she'd nonetheless light up various sections of grocers by what they'd assumed she chewed. Maternity nothing, her entire being seemed political. I'd find myself staring pleasantly at what had withered, what the years and erosion of matrimony had done to the woman. Nonetheless on occasion she'd flash a smile composed of concrete bits of living, and I knew that she did well.

Ted was tired. Never certain the cause I nonetheless—we—respected his disinterest. Spending one's time around the sleeping has its holy components. You know the dream is there, the possibility. A perpetual state of shift, Ted experienced. He might be any place. Medically though I'm uncertain, they'd flood him with some such and no one told us if that rendered dreams unlikely, or nightmares more certain. I'd watch him occasionally, though seldom. He had his twitches. I admired that about him, physically. The avoidance of atrophy. The tendency to jerk ourselves to waking if only to reassure our mind we haven't yet passed on. Our boy was near to death, I figured. I'd say as much while patrolling the home as a sort of sheriff. I made sure the entities kept on. I came from work awaft in grease. My mother would smile and hand me coffee. We'd sit there pondering the ebbs.

My father could be a nuisance in the truest sense. His tirades were Mussolinian. We lived thus in the dust of his leaving, trying to put together the pieces. Our home was stable, affordable. The neighbors entered and left with freedom and my mother knew each of their grandchildren's histories by heart. There was such weight amid these lives. Sister and mother were duly bitter as brother and I were fairly aloof. I'd spent the bulk of my youth awash in bathtubs reading strange stories in magazines about conspiracies. I'd wanted to study computer science, go someplace where I might fall asleep at my terminal making sense of codes that only made sense for seconds before being encrypted ad nauseam and torn to bits by teenaged masturbators. Passing, it looms over all of us in horrific ways. My father the tooth man the philanderer the arbiter of my homeland howled until you couldn't make out the words and eventually seemed to get bored enough to leave. That's all it was: a boredom. I remember looking over at my sister she was crying and asking whether we deserved a father, and he'd attempted to console and I just sat there wondering at paternity, fatherhood, the fatherland. My father had his German bearing. A naïve chauvinism maybe made him a proud American and thus he even looked the part of Nicolas Chauvin dawdling behind Napoleon and it was this that made him act the way he did, perhaps. The presidency, my father agape and sycophantic on each election day feeling the monotony of his daily works transcended by a dream of an America where drilling teeth held grave import. His fleeing then, political. An attempt to align his life with pundits. And then, no words.

    I say it now comfortably in retrospect as his entire face just seemed to smack of moneyed anger. His skin seemed pulled. I'd watch him smiling in various news stories. The donator. The giver. The philanthropist. Some drooling nineteen-year-old love slave hung across his whey-caked bicep. A nausea, then, in staring at my mother. This whole American spectrum. The lines between the figures in *American Gothic* and their import, the tines of his pitchfork, a family rent asunder by determined following. I'm not sure. One night my sister and I drove around listening to Stephen Wright albums and laughing. One night I read to my brother while he largely slept from Tolkien. One night I danced with my mother across the floor of our living room while on television a murder was investigated. If these are things that matter why the emptiness, largely, of our accounts?

I was a pink-fleshed boy and quite pathetic, I fucked up constantly when young and mostly tried to hide. Once I'd made a mistake and got myself stuck in the bathroom. I remember the sound as the walls closed in and my family pressed against them and my father became frustrated and pushed and kicked. I could hear each of them splitting and anger as I sat in a wretched puddle on the ground moaning. My skin was pink and deep red. There was bleeding. I could see the light above in blurs and tried to respond only to mumble nonsense and ask for help. I'd fallen on exiting the bathtub, the room flashed then with white tile and as I screamed out new pain shot through my leg as my father imposed his weight against the door. Just below my knee where rounded chalks of bone connected to shin or calf the door was thrust. I'd pulled the light on falling for balance and only slipped more fully into darkness as he shoved the structure hard into my skin. I felt it pulling at me and shouted out. I heard my mother's voice and discouragement, a calming. I laid there helpless in the dark my body curled and wet and strung. The world seemed to hold my leg inside its maw, clamped and metallic tastes rushed up my throat. I felt separated from the remainder of my leg, only a poisonous sting connected us. I felt vulnerable and raw and I flailed back and smashed my head against the tile. Everything closing in, my father hovering and mumbling something, my mother concerned. My body held there and as they're pushing lightly small winces ring out from me and my pink limbs. The room was freezing then, the house was always cold, everything as disordered as my frame as slowly I slid in darkness across the floor dragging wetted blood to offer entry. I remember my mother's face. I remember an inward horror. There are things more horrifying than a youthful loneliness and pain, but these were so pronounced they felt hallucinogenic. I was screaming out in pain and watching as my body lost its way yet further. My skin had gone from burning to freezing and the floor was wet with color. With each thrust it had wedged further until finally I'd slipped through and pulled my legs up to my chest and I felt entirely alone. I remember the swollen leg for days and my father's solemn attention to its care; the application of various medicines that left the thing shined and vulnerable, his various encouragements and cups of Tang. I could be such a meditative patient.

At one point, nearing on a month our family hadn't much seen Ted. We'd known where he was and that he'd eaten enough when we were sleeping, but something in the home itself seemed to cause his slip to rest. I couldn't figure. When your contacts are narrowed considerably the emotional drag they impose upon the heart tends to overwhelm. Ted was sleeping pulling each heart toward his forested hell.

Our neighbor was Carl. Carl had lost his wife; found a dog. He hadn't done much in the last years but engage his mind with television. I admired the man. Ted, when conscious, had always spoken highly of their talks. Ted used to walk that way with our former pet and stop for minutes of conversation. One night Carl made his way into my mother's kitchen complaining of pained chest, something. We were each asleep, excepting Ted, I later learned. Carl stumbled in on Ted swallowing handsful of dry cereal. His eyes black sockets. His stomach sunken in. Ted looked sickly, freshly freed from being locked away. I'd seen him later in the hospital and noted the odd markings along the ridges of his hands. They seemed distended and warped, bad Dali replicas or Nosferatus, he reached toward Carl once as the sun shone through hospital shade and it seemed to look clean through to Ted's blood. Red marks along from forearm to the very edge of that vampiric pointer finger. It was the first time I'd registered sympathy in Ted's physique in years.

So Carl had entered my mother's kitchen to discover my inept Ted. The two of them stared apparently until Ted's conscience overwhelmed; an ambulance then called. Each of us at rest the home might've as easily been Carl's casket. The home might've burned to dust, upped and fled on my father's way. I'm uncertain; it doesn't matter. As Ted reached out under bad hospital light I imagined the conversations they ought to have had there. The awkward gestures. Carl reaching toward his heart. Ted attempting to convey what he'd been up to over the months. Neither of them succeeding, both of them suffering. Carl's eyes were sunken too, a match for Ted. My mother brought his yapping rat and Carl seemed unhappy to see it, only continuing to vent to Ted just what he'd seen, just what he'd missed. A widower, a male, his children up and gone, my mother just a reach or toss from all his windows. My mother, left, aging, sickly, unfortunate, weary and disgusted at most things. The two of them made logical mates, but neither saw as much. Ted seemed to know it at times, I remember that. He'd reach out for alternate fathers as Ellen sought my mom. This incestuous inward looking, it spread to everything. I, Frederick, held no sway inside my mind, merely subject to the waxes and wanes of home and its rooms.

I spat once on my boss's fancy car. It wasn't out of spite but curiosity. I don't know whether anyone notices anything. The jury is ever out, you might've guessed. I'm on this medication that makes my teeth feel deprived, barren. I can barely hawk spit to save face and yet that day walking by en route home from greased employ I leant away for dear life like some pitcher's last stand and let what felt my whole gut's contents on the driver's window, the soft convertible's roof, and wherever else I couldn't see. I'm not sure what occurred thereafter but my imagination knew multitudes. Endless possibilities of his dissatisfaction. My stomach gets hot over the various materials we use to heat the families' repasts. There's nothing glorious about it, just sequential movement. We inch and inch. Of late Ted's been up and about a bit, not much though. I yearn for Carl but he never much took to my conversation. His heart ought to persist. We search for parental figures. This is not about a youth.

BOREDOMS

I'm a better tabloid than citizen. What I mean is I prefer a basement. I live to run away. A friend of mine once wound up on the cover of their city's weekly having passed out near the lawnmower he worked. He'd fixed up nearby within a building for soil and various landscaping tools and nodded off on a hillside holding his penis. I met him in treatment. Wonderful fellow, informed me of my bisexuality. He'd left one day for court and returned with pornography flat against his belly, tucked and sweated within jeans. He'd exhumed it and hatched a plot to scoop away the ceiling's makeup and tunnel into the female rooms. Always in fantasy. Always these glorious days. I hid that night seated on the shower's curtain while it ran, my foot wedged beneath the door so as to stop intruders. We weren't allowed locks. We weren't allowed spiral notebooks. We weren't allowed even the slightest suicidal material. Some cut themselves with spoons they'd dug into bricks or concrete for an edge. My method of barricading sometimes left massive red scrapes on my feet and others would hide, compulsive, on the floor—their backs against the door—to compensate. I'm always compensating. I grin often and phonily. For a stretch there I could be quite obsessive. I'm not in treatment any longer.

On leaving I discovered circles of likeminded fuckups not comfortable in therapy and we'd formed groups who'd caused eruptions of boring discord. A Midwestern colifata, I imagined. Always apologizing for weeping over our fathers, always qualifying any time our ramble went overlong. First I'd gone to the university and spraypainted *NEVER WORK* repeatedly down its walls. I felt guilt later but couldn't figure a way through. Poor workers are often suffering the whims of idiots such as me. Then a friend and I we'd freed a slew of kept animals. I preferred this sort of mission in mostly every sense. My friend spent the night drinking and howling as was his wont, I followed the animals I kept pace with ensuring they were not hit by cars, ambling furry masses of potential yipping and sprinting at lights. I listened for the howl of my friend and I attempted to corral the animals toward it though eventually I saw fit to collapse and give my friend the night alone. I woke up sunburnt in weeds near a highway and spent the morning trying to fashion materials with which to write. I always found comfort in the sun, the pressures of my sinuses would dissipate and I might lay on my back floating in some creek. I tend to worship the sun. If there's religion for me that's the closest. I'd read of Thelema a bit here and there and been drawn in by Thee Temple Ov Psychick Youth. I was fond of the notion of a spiritual order established firmly awash in television. I was fond of the balance of tyranny and freedom. I was fond of their family lives, their constant experimentation, the ritual. We'd each of us read of it in turn and tried to make such a life for us. We shaved one another's heads and burned our palms with upturned candles' wax. It was a journey inward and all of us were making work. Occasionally we'd blur and this was the purest state.

 I did work, and it didn't suit me, and I don't recommend it. When I met Ivan and his ilk, then, my mind was dense with possibility. Ivan had worked for radio stations mostly, hosting shows a bit or cleaning up, holding fundraisers or conducting yearly festivals. Through this he'd managed to start a minor label primarily made up of Japanese noise acts and solitary rural black metalish recording artists who'd likely have taken to terrorism were it not for whatever this was. Ivan was a good person and not quite a person. Ivan did was he felt compelled to do. I observed him mostly. I'd attended regional shows where fey androgynous blondes might punch guitars to spray their blood and hooded art students might conduct some throb on destroyed drum machines. The appeal of the show was the opportunity to bleed, to scream, to kneel and grind one's forehead into the concrete without judgment. I've taken months of therapy that couldn't come close. These were my kind. When morning came for us the floor was covered in bodies. Cigarettes burned and were passed from hand to hand. Greased hair and jeans unbuttoned on the floor in warmth and us rolling over and making jokes. We slept that way long into the afternoon and one of us would rise to make us coffee. Sharing a certain state with others has a profound effect on what one can accept for living. We evaded reality together. We squeezed every bit of every penny together. We went swimming in the river in the sun and talked endlessly. We fell in love.

Ivan recorded the shows meticulously and shared them online for interested drooly-mouthed depressives. He sold albums, either on tape or seven inch vinyl he'd pay to have pressed when money existed. Mostly this meant nothing was released but when it was you'd hear it whispered at and slowly cults might build. We were reading about groups like Les Rallizes Dénudés or figures like Atrax Morgue. We were listening to power electronics on shifts at print shops or Einstürzende Neubaten in ratty cars with near-strangers who offered drugs. I largely abstained but never held it over anybody. I was testing myself. I was trying. I remember the song of living thus. I remember Ivan driving wildly in sprawling fields and my arms out the window and I'm vomiting against the hull of his truck. I remember the abrasive yelling and the field recordings and the women and the men in light and fucking around or pulling at parts or laying on blankets in pure dark and having some connection to the ether, the sound. It was a feeling to welcome and hold against your breast. It was an oilsoaked bird plucked from a poisoned ocean singing at your heart. These were the people I came to love, and held.

This was the nature of the thing: youths without desire for parents hunched over in rooms while longheld droning notes pushed them and they pushed back. A sound became an opportunity to fight, a primal scream at some grinding tool and winning out. Escape, escape. Some were older, I was older. I was old by some standard and always felt unease until the noise came. My friends and I we'd get in fights and get called empty by the cops who'd break them up. Always this fight against the cop within, always some screaming. They were right but we were searching. We'd fight one another by various rivers and fall in laughing while night slouched its dullard way to day. I was always staring at the sun. I was always needy. I prayed for burning sun and sand. I wanted to lose my heart. I don't care for bands but experiences. I want to be your dog. I have long teeth and people look at me quick to turn and change their mind. We fed our heads on slews of chemicals and having eradicated one possibility moved on to tempered, acceptable rebellions. Vans filled with lust and yelling, trucks veering away from dawn. Bands worked. People were desperate to make these bands perform. We were desperate to watch them harm themselves. Someone played Throbbing Gristle in the background. Someone shouted about their father. Someone took in a rail of meth. Someone punched a wet hard surface. Someone screamed through teethed guitar strings into pickups. Someone fucked the floor. Always someone being. Nobody could judge. We did our best Ian Curtis impressions. People bought generators and stole generators and found fields far enough away where bands would play in cold. We'd circle up what cars we had to bob and hobble into one another swelling and contracting with the music. It wasn't about longevity or rejection, it was about the sense of fabric against your skin and knowing it might rip but pushing and quieting the language in your head. Their leather jackets made me weep. Their putrid hugs felt like a thousand mothers. It wasn't about relating but still existed this primal nag to dress and stitch clothes together while dying down in all too human smelling basements in the day.

We wore an armor then, were called various things and screamed at from cars driven by put together males. We laid in beds in morning together and were photographed by one of us. We laid there on the floor in someone's home and tried to convert them. We talked about the future and leaving the city for something else. We went to public libraries for research. I read from newspapers for opportunities. I read from manuals on survival for our keep. I read to them from *Dhalgren* and didn't understand and it didn't matter. I wanted to feel free and they were freeing. I wanted to embrace them and shut something out. I wanted to take in the world and the citizen and the criminal and the putrid and make it my own, make it something lit and hearty in the sun. I talked to them about my imaginary siblings. I talked to them about the past. I talked to them about a place we all might go. We fucked one another and welcomed the escape. The basements seemed to call to us and always this noise and fight. Always this skepticism of control. Always this disavowal, apostasy, whatever. Always this crowd of thought and bother. Always the mornings bright and whole. I'll wander sometimes looking for their sounds. I'll leave my home and search out for what never existed. A bit of extra bleach drops on a T-shirt and I wince. I miss them every day.

EVERYBODY'S DARLING

My mother the masochist, my mother the manuscript. Returning always to places and people she'd said rotted away her guts. My not-aunt Lila and the notion of a family stitched together through traumas. My mother volunteering in cities and bringing home women offering refuge from the fists of men. My mother singing to us kids while we sat on the stairway awaiting dinner. My mother gleaming in the courtrooms as I sat in back making notes on homework or reading stories. My mother a hopeless open demeanor in the face of stern Texas indifference and longstanding racism along the borders. I am my mother. I am sickened by the world of today, what I do with myself.

Hope is not a feeling I care for. My mother's place in Houston was lined with red brick and bright green flora she'd said had climbed the building since the late nineteenth century.

I found her in a state when I arrived and all I could do was pace outside her home those nights greedily choking down

Salem after Salem. She'd taken certain materials from her past and strewn them about the living area: old records smeary with dust or globs of gum, receipts slid into their lining, T-shirts from various colleges in fading oranges and reds, empty bottles of French wine and sunglasses she'd prided since I was young from Greece, a military jacket she said she'd stolen from the floor of Terry Southern's New York place after they'd listened all night to reports of violence everywhere. There she'd sit on a tufted leather couch either prattling on the phone to a team of law students assembling and managing her casework or picking up piece after piece of history, using each to expand my sense of who she'd been.

My mother grew up in Pennsylvania. Awake I guess to the dull fabric of the fifties, my mother donned suede leathers in 1965—I'll wear them, I'll wear them.

"Be well, Homer. Take care of those you love." Her name was Henrietta and once my mother told me she'd helped Jean Genet find a clean shave in Chicago before he was to speak. This was 1968 and after meeting Bernardine Dohrn my mother had taken to militancy—I hold in my hand a bullet she'd been given by Genet's lover. "Ever the criminal. Ever the artist. Ever the American."

Thinking of her now, I have no use for writing—only assembly. To write, to sit here and write out some words to make you look—I have no use for it. Language is useless that way. The minute you stop to figure what it is you're only lost in more of it. Families are worse that way, small gesturing bodies of language you want to make sense of, forget it. Your mother you love, worship even, you're sick and sycophantic after her. Your father you hate, wonderful. Great work. I'm the same.

We don't tell ourselves stories for reasons. We invent gods and makers who forced it on us. The Egyptians, sure. But what do I care for Ancient Egypt? Worship cats, sure. Another word. Another badly hewn sentence on the people's grave. I like it, sure. My mother named me Homer because before he'd left my father told her stories. She wanted a name strong enough to lock the doors if he returned. My father had anger.

I'm not an artist, I promise. I'm not even really suffering. Just talked too much to Sissy about it all so I'm second-guessing the whole bit.

People are bad, I say, it's what my mother often said. Her father used to lay into them and feel her up a bit so soon as she could my mom made for streets elsewhere and built a life—slowly, slowly. Ten years after my mom finished law school in a dull auditorium while my aunt Lila—not my real aunt—held an anxious whining me upon her lap, watching. I felt raised amid women, maybe. We drove to Pennsylvania to visit her mother, my grandma, as her father was locked away for strangling his second wife so she lost all means of speech, forever. My father and Sissy stayed home in Texas as my parents were beginning the first of several forays to the outs. We visited and dipped our feet into Lake Erie. My mother detested her home and spent the drive talking about various communes she'd stayed in from rural Wisconsin towns of dullards, down through the outskirts of Chicago where the metropolis sent its young to revolt and fuck within the dirt in the Summer of Love.

I liked my grandmother well enough. She told me, she said, *Homer, Keep well away from these tickertape parades you'll see for this America—it isn't hardly America anymore.*

Old racist, I figured, and took to having long walks on roads of Amish buggies jutting my own mangled arms out to passers-by and hiccupping the pledge of allegiance to the fourth reich of syrup, dumb dawdling landscape.

I suppose I took to mother's unders when the end became too sure. Our parents couldn't live forever—a naive dream, and I, a little dog, I yipped foolishly about the house ensuring her safety while life left her bones and fingertips and Multiple Sclerosis stopped us cold. I'd packed up life and limb and moved to Houston when her coughing got to me. We'd speak on the phone and she'd tell sprawling stories of her lives while I paced a small plot of grass outside of my apartment. I'd lived in Decatur, Illinois and entered data for four nauseating years. Work, thus, on turning south, brought only minor sport and headache to get. That first night I arrived we two drank vodka infinitum watching Sophia Loren shout carelessly at Marcello Mastroianni from a prison's window.

Over time she'd stitched together a family's history for me, and I was grateful. I'd forgotten much of what I've only just started to transcribe.

I have never wanted to live as an artist. My mother I'm uncertain. Growing up I remember her railing against Patty Hearst long after the world had forgotten. Children, she thought. Establish a community, work to get better. Build families based on love, not convenience. Not even love of convenience. She'd make these asides while we watched mysteries on TV or I gathered her medicine and I've assembled them on old receipts and napkins as her life, my story.

Chant, un chant, my mother amid the swell of bodies in Chicago being beaten at the hands of Daley sneering, angry, bulbous. Wherever she's lived my mother seemed to occupy and claim an ownership of her cities. The later years of her life she'd engaged in tumult in Texas people still mumble at in cop bars. Her life in the '60s brought about such waves of stupor and sorrow that she didn't finish law school until 1979, working all the while with me in tow, my father then a cop with mustache. They'd returned to Pennsylvania where they lived in a home well outside the city but she studied at Temple, driving in some mornings well before dawn to teach, study, teach, study. My grandmother watched me and all day we'd spend in the yard with pups.

I felt myself foraging, is what it was. You encounter death and your body does strange things. Halls in the home are stuck with meaning, dragged out as dull conversations with the dead. I'd walk through her room and run my fingers beneath necklaces strung over vanity mirrors I hadn't had the presence of mind to turn out.

It was several weeks after she'd died and the funeral's dust had settled that I'd started to dig through dressers. Wherever she'd lived my mother had anointed each space with an ornate touch of laces and glass that made one tiptoe. On previous visits before her turn I'd always felt it necessary to walk on eggshells and keep my vulgar habits at bay. I'd hawk and spit and belch within my rented car while picking up her medicine. Now that she'd gone I felt those urges ripped from me. Whatever desire previous had made me want to yell and assert my living upon the scene had vanished, quiet, as though it never existed.

One day near the end, early, I'd gone to work to pick up my check. There were minor tasks I'd do involving the digitizing of either transcripts from local business meetings with the city council or entering handwritten notes for various legal professionals who'd developed agreements with my boss. It was fulfilling work in that at the beginning I was handed a large number of something that I'd then process and see altered, but truth be told I'd found myself wanting to return to school.

    So I'd picked up my check and cashed it at a bank in downtown Houston amid heat and bodies bound up in suits with jowly men and women whose makeup seemed sturdier than the skin beneath, their eyes simultaneously glorious with color while sunken, their hair pulled up and blonde as if in shrieking horror from the skin: tanned it was and often sad as leather. I worshiped these women.

My mother had told me of meeting Bernardine Dohrn on a campus in Wisconsin where they'd smoked and bellowed hymnal chants while being nudged by the knees of frustrated university police. This warped into a trip in a van over a week or so through sleepy Wisconsin towns and campuses until arriving in Chicago for the Democratic National Convention. She'd fallen out with the Weather Underground and wound up wandering through Lincoln Park kicking leaves when suddenly she heard a straining William Burroughs reciting the menu of a nearby diner he'd stolen, vomited upon, and declared the opening to his next novel.

I think of the fact that I am intruding—I am an intruder—and how unsavory she'd find it. It's scatterbrained, sure, but my mother had certainly established an ethic of her own over the course of her living, a sense of authenticity I guess, a fuller self. I opened the top drawer of a massive darkwood chest and saw them. A sea of pinks and whites, offwhites and yellows. Silk, lace, fabrics apparently having conversations with one another and yet the whole thing a wonderful plot of calm, a wave of sleep. I pulled in a pile as many of the laundered unders I could grab and threw them gleeing onto the bed. I didn't jump backward trusting, but fell face-forward into the minor mass of history and for the first time since my mother's death was capable of sleep. I burrowed into them as small blankets, serviettes of warmth.

Before being conscious of it my brain stopped—I am full.

Growing up I'd puttered after my mother fawning. She'd been the DA in Houston twenty years before my deadbeat ratfaced father took Sissy on to California. I continue to speak at length with Sissy but wrote the old man off long before he'd left—he had a brazen presence, would walk about in utilitarian clothes yawping about local elections, that sort of thing, all the while working a miniscule stretch of hours cleaning classrooms and emptying garbages at the university. Easy would've been he'd died first, cordial. This was not the stubborn bastard's way, alas, so close to mom I'd stuck.

My mother made of light and standing hand in hand with Abbie Hoffman to levitate the Pentagon. My mother spitting on riot shields on Michigan Avenue as beaten bodies are hauled off. My mother scolding my father for his chauvinism toward America, the president, his blind worship of an ideal. My mother in suits and dresses. My mother in communes and secondhand flowery drapes. My mother holding me in rain as we watched our family split. My mother in makeup, in jewelry, in tatters having married the same man who'd ruined her childhood, in circles of protest and telling stories to empty rooms, courts, fireplaces while Sissy and I bounced anxious on her lap.

After weeks of whatever it was I had a troubling discussion with my Sissy about the world. I'd stopped going to work and spent my days smoking on my mother's bed in robes reading the late journals of Jean Cocteau.

"I have no interest in anything, Sissy. Sometimes I wish for things, hopes that you and I and mom had made our way west instead of how it went. This has all been so tiring. Mother had so many ties in this city. The mail just piles up and I'm overwhelmed with all I'd never know about her."

"Are you actually thinking of staying on in Houston, Homer?"

"Yes. I don't know. Why?"

"We've talked about this, if memory serves. You shouldn't bury yourself in this sort of grief over a woman who never wanted to be known."

"You don't know what you're talking about. *That's him.* That's his voice in your throat in spite. She left it all for me to know her."

"That's crazy! She was just as rotten as he was! Do you even remember when you left home?"

"Everyone leaves home. Leaving home's important, Sissy."

"That was reality, Homer. You hardly spoke for weeks and all you'd do was sit on my couch watching movies!"

"I was content, Sissy. I was happy. I knew where I stood in this world because of her. I connected with history."

"Oh bullshit. You know better than anyone that half the stuff she talked about was secondhand garble from her reading. Our mother was a dull old bat with—"

"Stop it Sissy! Stop talking like this!"

"—nothing and she. Stop what?"

"Don't talk. There's nothing to say. I'm so sick of these eulogies."

"I'm trying to help you, Homer. Her presence is a sickness. You can't stay there."

"I'm staying here. None of it makes any difference, Sissy."

"You never sleep. You lose your mind in all of it."

"You're our father's daughter. I'm my mother's son. We are doomed."

"Our parents aren't that fucking important! They're just as fucked up and useless as we've been."

"I remember the first time she read to us, Sissy. The floor was covered in materials for that murder—*the trial of her life*, the mantra—and she'd picked up a bit of Poe and read to us until we slept, foreheads pressed, against her chest."

"This doesn't matter, Homer. You need to leave Houston."

"I need to be a body. I need to leave and join the working world. I need to right my head. I need to shake loose mother's garbage. I'm a wandering dog. I am an idiot. I miss you, Sissy."

"I don't think I've ever wanted to know our parents, Homer. All that yelling and violence and useless expended energy. Why would you pursue that?"

"I didn't pursue anything, Sissy. These people. You never knew the mom I knew. Her teeth sunk into you, bigger than life, all she had to do was hack up a bit on the phone and I was down here applying for work."

"Have you talked to anybody but me since she died, Homer?"

"I've done what I can. This house gets to me some days. How many fucking lavender-scented devices could our mother have possibly owned?"

My mother a series of outfits hung in closets and various stages of undress or preparation between the many lives she held. My mother a beacon of strength, of fire, of anger at strains of the status quo. An American, an artist, a criminal. I'm not sure why it sticks out. Time spent at Texas's Gulf of Mexico in the water and my mother tanned and polkadotted even adrift in the sea of shit her life seemed to amass around her. My mother and father sharing beers seated in the car and all of us sunburnt and tired as we waited for bags of breaded fast food shrimp.

Arguably, life and all its mires, family and all its rot, it in turn leads to bodies; the stuff we press to self to feel less dead or bored. I wear a dress and ask a question of establishing an identity that makes me want to leave her home and seek company, and the question of physical sprawl as we crawl like slugs across a floor of tortures hoping to evoke something stronger than tugs at skin or worse. My mind is circling itself. I hate my self. Return then to the beginning, origins, a need for multiple bodies in one to even feel content on earth, perhaps, or simply the genuine spiritual belief that this is so. I carry my mother. I love my mother. I adore my mother.

It's fine. There's something else. I find myself reading of genderless maniacs and men in dresses. I cannot believe Sissy. I am Rrose Selavy. Cover yourself in gold and abrade your face. Watch footage of what a family might've been and set the film on fire.

The day after my mother died I found myself seated in a room in a hospital being asked questions about the particulars of her existence. I wanted to vomit. I wanted to take this awful feeling in my gut and put it to some kind of use. I wanted to watch my mother live and know my mother, Henrietta. I wanted to ask her every question about every day she'd lived and feel complete. We draw connections with our parents. We need our parents and sometimes their need of us as carriers of torches is lost. We become disappointments, dull, unambitious citizens who haven't found our way. For a long while afterward I went about like this. Asleep at work to the noise of what life asked of me. Asleep at home avoiding my mother's room. I come away without feeling much relief or hope for what might be for me, only connecting more and more to what she'd left behind. I pace the hardwood floors in robes and silk and watch the days transpire. I answer mail. I touch up my makeup in mirrors and listen to records. I have wasted my life. I think of why a body might sit down to get one's thoughts out rather than simply end it. I can't speak with Sissy about it as our parents seem to have successfully convinced each of us of something in the other. I can't go to work and I can't establish friendships. I think of Sophia Loren's apparent relief having entered prison in that film—prior they'd had child after child as a loophole to avoid being locked away. The language, the mess, the ties of family and all make a mild prison established for oneself suddenly seem immensely more appealing than living. I dress then not to make some new connection with the world, but to sever it. I put on lingerie and see my balding, unkempt flesh in mirrors mother had strewn about and feel at one with my complete botching of reality. I smoke Salem after Salem and watch television and fill myself with foods and hear her fabrics stretch and rip at rest upon the couch and I am calm, I am a lifeless gleam in mother's eye.

DRAIN SONGS
A NOVELLA

"I do not plead, I merely produce documents, for and against"

—*Opium*, Jean Cocteau

"And set up instead a random craving for images. If drugs weren't forbidden in America, they would be the perfect middle-class vice. Addicts would do their work and come home to consume the huge dose of images awaiting them in the mass media. Junkies love to look at television. Billie Holiday said she knew she was going off drugs when she didn't like to watch TV. Or they'll sit and read a newspaper or magazine, and by God, read it all. I knew this old junkie in New York, and he'd go out and get a lot of newspapers and magazines and some candy bars and several packages of cigarettes and then he'd sit in his room and he'd read those newspapers and magazines right straight through. Indiscriminately. Every word."

—William Burroughs

A handful of intoxicant platitudes bound in leather. Hold fast to your texts. Use them. A people reduced to affirmatives and negatives, nods, and spending their mornings at counters overconscious. What can the human animal become addicted to? Everything. Watchful ranks of anxiety, overseers, parents, caretakers, sponsors, people to set things right, things to set right people. A grave, a massive weeping and one of them listening to the final moments of Jonestown, wondering at parallels. Perhaps the human being needs its cult. Perhaps the whole of humanity is its cult. Charismatic leaders, doctrine, efficacy. Paperwork, organizations, institutions, good days. Sad suited white men in Akron. Doctors, wives, children, pets, mistresses, clichés. A donation struck for living, to keep the deaths at bay. Wallow a bit in heaves of spirituality. Accept. What can the human animal become addicted to? Histories of idols who've opened their palms for us. First name last initial. New here. Trying this out. Peopled stairwells in rehabilitation centers climed of smoke. A cap and gown of solitude for years of bereavement, titles and ways of coping, methods and secrets writ on toilet walls for loners, speech therapy and art therapy and hydrotherapy and primal therapy and we'll go by pseudonyms protecting innocence. By means of spirituality, what can you do to communicate with others when you feel the disadvantages of your forebears. It's genetic. It's in your blood. It's in your putrid genes. It's always there. You can't escaped it. First you watched aunts and uncles stumble around pathetic and drunk. Now they're lecturing you. You were capable, then the loss of sanity, and what always works. I'll be your mirror. I'll be your tourniquet. I'll listen to you over the phone that's mounted to the wall. I'll leave you and you'll be escorted back to your unit. I want you to be O.K. I want you to be happy. I want you to feel better. You're an addict, an alcoholic. You're insatiable. You would've taken anything to shut off your brain. You would've taken everything to make things quiet. You're obsessed. You're depressed. You're anxious. You're paranoid. You're making life impossible for me. I understand. I need you to understand. I'm an addict. I'm an alcoholic. I'm caught in something. I'll attend the classes. I'll watch the TV specials. I'll watch the TV. I'll binge. I'll take every cure. I'll live with monks. I'll live in a camp and be abused in Montana. I'll do anything. I don't want to die. I can't keep going like this. I don't want to die.

ONE

"This was not memory-loss, there was some damage of course to his celebrated memory but not much: this was delusion. And now it had taken over, again. One might shroud one's head. Forever. He felt—depressed."

—*Recovery*, John Berryman

He leaves his home near campus, beery breath and notes follow; he clinks within a glassine liquor marveling at vitrines of forget. A pipe loads, becomes smoked. He'd been interviewed in multiple capacities and begun his novel. *Recovery* would be a treatise to complicate Henry and Mr. Skull & Bones. He felt leaden and empty. The winters in Minnesota were sorrowful. Saul was transcribing his likeness. He stood on the corner and watched the evolution of snow to mud. A bridge, some fabric in wind. Skin on face dry and hair bristling uncomfortably. Mind awash in language, image, boredom. A simple white wooden chair on which to sit and bed one's woes for good. He wondered. His eyes sunken in beneath the plastic frame and he's worn holed socks inside an elderly pair of Florsheims that hug his ankles yet chafe when he steps too readily. His coat swallows air around him and to see him coming you'd worry at what length of accosting might ensue. He'd wavered and wavered and raised hands maniacally against various podia lamenting the word, the boredom, the utter utter boredom of every bit of breathing. It was closing in on him. Today he'd fled earlier than typical and soon the wife would question, interrogate. He remembered the feeling of interrogating E. at St. Elizabeth's, of trying to ascertain just where the work might lead for him. Already though the fascism had left his grimace, what remained was mere vocal wandering. Pound the saint reduced to his demoniacal inkling. He had great contempt for all his schooling, all this schooling. He could stand before some lot of undergraduates vying and sleep on feet while prattling on toward Keats or Coleridge, a deadness, a boozy wettened deadness emanating at all of them like so many rips in their potential. The students, the citizenry. The Middle-West a plaguey place for drunks and liars. He wanted to scream. He hoped to scream out. Nothing was adequate for what ailed him. No bottle was large enough. No poem was sound enough. No classroom was filled enough. His hands were damp with sweat. His hands. His eyes looked wild and he barely kept it together during hours in his office when he smoked and stared at the wall and wrote in the margins of his desk copy of Poe's collected tales.

You are searching for something. Hence the assemblage. Hence the curiosity toward both past depressives, opioid addicts, abusers, maniacs, drunks, and the mass of interpretations you've found toward Dürer. We have no means of reaching it beyond the fictive, the indirect, the imagistic. It would look like a newly-sober addict's notebook. It wouldn't look right. You've crudely amassed notes then. Notes crudely amassed. Therapies and anecdotes. Recordings illegal, breaches. Things taken that were not supposed to be taken that would slight the dignity of those if they'd known. You are a liar, in a community of liars. You are home. There is only fiction. This is your assertion. Analyzing Alan Severance as a means of this. Analyzing the addict and the alcoholic not as stable identities but as sociocultural clichés, symptoms of a much longer misery. The assemblage, a pretentious lot of sniveling and navel-gazing. You are making a map, attempting to beget coherence. It is impossible. Preoccupy yourself with drunks and mumblers. Listen to whatever sounds they've made. Put it into its packaging. Was he a drunk? The bulbous gut of Orson Welles and hedonism's end in the twentieth century. Screened waves of gluttony. Information overload. A tendency within society to swill before the collapse. Roman festivals of shit and wine, blood. You observe and render opinions. You are having an off decade.

"My friend he tells me any number of things to get me to shut the fuck up. I can't keep with it. The world is sorrow. I've listened to stories in here. I've listened to each and every one of you tell me something or other about what's gone on, how you've come to be, and this person can't listen to me for five fucking minutes about what I'm going through?" (Nods, identification, encouragement, fidgets) "We're driving home from work, you know? I have to say something anyway. I have to talk on drives, man, you know? I have to keep my thoughts *out*side my head in that motherfucker. I cannot get too alone, especially if I'm just about to get home? Nothing but a TV waiting for me? So that's what brings me here. Come here, say something, find out what's what, I dunno, I just had to speak. I just wanted to tell that friend what he meant to me. How I'd never have got clean without him. How my whole life I got together a group of shithead dopefiend friends and threw them out for you all and that's great—that's great, don't mistake me—but I just want to tell this guy what it means he let me be his friend, come into his home, just be *normal* around him. Can't happen, I'm discouraged and back at home quick in front of that TV. All suddenly I know this is where I need to be, so I go. I hit a meeting. I commune. I communicate. This fucking head, man. It wants me dead. It wants me deep underground, no longer thinking, no longer aware. I think it's me most days. My head isn't me. I don't know how to put this. I don't know what to say. My fucking head just wants me dead." (The evening comes to a close shortly thereafter, chairs are folded and hands are shook, two newcomers receive sponsors, literature purchased, coffee drunk, the room becomes a backroom in a church again and all these lives tiptoe back to the working world)

(Termed a *gaggle* these older ladies assemble breakfasts from kitchens and bakeries across the city, people stumble in mumbling, some clad ready with cellphone strapped on hip in leather case, others hold *Daily Meditation* texts and read over them mouthing the words to themselves and closing eyes when appropriate, later, dissatisfied patchbearded M. addresses the group re: his status) "My mother won't find it. You hear that? Always I've walked about this way, I used to carry a picture of my father to inspire me, no more. He died pissing himself the same amount in his bank account as when forty years old. Different generation, them. Family mattering. I've gone deadbeat on one kid won't dare fuck this one up. All this time though I keep seeing my mother's face and imagine what she'd hoped for. After my father passed she'd sit for hours just staring out. Eventually what happens she mumbles to me about looking endlessly for what makes life whole, life worth living. I hide my guns. She was a depressive woman, my mother. Could perform. Often she'd commiserate with father about the end times, that sort and such. But I'd never heard her talk that way, so goddamn *sad*. These walls, whatever they say, however this place got here, it seems tied up in that, the guts of this old woman muttering at the ends. It's impossible to know, but maybe that's our problem in here. Never accepting the impossibility, never accepting the not knowing… I want to go outside now… I want to leave and I want not come back for awhile. I say this but I don't feel it. I feel like I don't feel anything of late. I take medications that're supposed to help. I know some of you feel off about that. I've tried. I've tried so many things I can't keep them straight. I look around and just want it to stop, want to feel better, want to feel alive. I'll be in the gas station staring off into light and somebody will have to pull me from that state. I'll be at work—I sell cars, you knew this—and suddenly the whole room will seem to press in on my head. *This isn't meds*, I'll tell myself. *This isn't how chemicals make you feel, they aren't political.* I'm on a date and suddenly my hands will start to sweat, it all seems bound up in what she said, this ongoing fucking misery thing, never ending it's always there. I can't think. (Abrasive tension as hands are patted upon his back and the room continues in its circles as the morning members have their shares and sip their coffees, some return to halfway houses on finishing the start, some head off to work or home, all tired, all feeling the weight of their ideas)

She'd been hospitalized for several weeks intermittently. It was complicated. She was suspected of forms of neglect and such. She recorded these things as best she could and publicized them on her release. It felt like a gesture toward being famous. She didn't care about that. She didn't care about money as she'd never had to think on it. She cared about some feeling that seemed to be living in her gut from when she turned nineteen or so. Dürer's work came in after the handing over of her child to her parents while putting certain things back in order. She loved her and saw her frequently but felt as if she was invading the space of their relationship whenever around. She'd focused heavily on the biographies of certain artists and their absenteeism at fatherhood. It seemed to make matters cohere but still left that fleeing gut concern. His works, his engravings, his takes on humanity and the artist within humanity's movement helped a bit and she considered her efforts in smearing shades as aligned with redemption of failures. She was obsessive, would take anything to slow her down, a case study to overpaid psychiatrists, an opportunity to publish. What then. Is she a cliché? There is a world of cliché burying her in its wake and all she'll contribute to the slush is a crackling ahem. Ahem there's more to it than that. Ahem I don't deserve this. Ahem I'm trying hard not to fail. Ahem I've been clean for several days. She's trying hard to assemble something with the work and her writing and the images and the past and her walking but drink and depression and medication and failure and sopping wet heaps of rejected works have created a perfect wall between what might be and her hands. A boy walks by with father hooked in hand and for a moment she feels tempted to weep. She can't but it isn't significant. She hasn't and hasn't expected to cry in some time. Life has been reduced to occasional sketches on the backs of prescriptions standing in line at CVS while the light seems to eat away at her flesh. What chemicals would most quickly stupefy? What combination might I sneak into the family bathroom for a nap? Might I get a ride to a mall and drink cough syrup to watch the seniors? How can I escape?

"I always loved these flowers; they emanate, you know? Full of energy. Since working there I've just come to love this; the oils, all these smells. I have so many projects, so much to do. I pulled a friend away from relapsing last weekend. She'd gone out with an old boyfriend who shoved his foot into her back one night when they were full up. I pulled her out of that place by hair and took her along the street to where this calm old fellow played his songs. It never stops for anyone I knew. They've all persisted and it hasn't mattered how they saw me or what OD they pulled me from. They would stretch a week of my use over a lifetime of lost weekends and I am just here. I'm here. I have to meet new people here. The calm old fellow played us something over and over and I held her hair and petted it and put one of these flowers along her ear and dripped oil on her too; she was full of fear. I could see it. I have no way of connecting with men anymore. She's the only person I'd felt pulled enough to leave my place and drive to where she'd lost it. We smoked my cigarettes and the calm old fellow played his songs long into the night and I had her sleep on my couch. It was nothing special. I just loved to hear her being when we woke."

There were times—and no one said as much—that sobriety became a kind of limit-experience. Pushed, apparently, beyond the reach of chemical release from living, there'd often be moments where simply avoiding pills, avoiding liquor stores, was sufficient. Some might visit the parking garage downtown and walk along its ledge, potential death right there but staying. Some might read obsessively, checking out hundreds of books from various libraries, watching foreign films. Many, and J.B. was apparently no different, sought release through artwork. Prison writing programs and organizations offering art therapy. It's not exactly that, though, is what I'm saying. It isn't art therapy, it goes beyond this. It's present-tense mythologizing of oneself. It's performative. These people aren't simply whiteknuckling and avoiding fucking up because they can see the result just on the horizon and know it'll be worth the struggle. They're narrating. They're creating stories to save themselves. Some exaggerate. Most exaggerate. They all do it though. They become soldiers of sorts in a larger struggle. No atheists in foxholes perhaps. Though this isn't always spiritual. It isn't about kneeling before god for all of them. Some suffer hard and sit within their cars in parking lots looking at diners where they'd eaten thinking massive vacuumed thoughts and tossing shots back at the void. Some need to make themselves into martyrs but most would be embarrassed to publicly acknowledge it. It surfaces in bathetic yawps. "What about my sobriety!" "Yeah but at least I'm still sober!" And it never feels quite how it does inside coming out. The point is these are lives. The point is since the dawn human animals have sought some sort of internal quiet. Whatever these individuals are they aren't merely thoughtless gluttons. They're just hardwired to see the quiet as far better than any noise we've lobbied against the potential of nonexistence. Again, death. It grows as a preoccupation for most and perhaps anybody until we become too demented to remember our firstnames and then we're close enough to dream it. An emptiness, being. I keep a copy of Sade next to my big book and twelve and twelve and tend to fall somewhere in the middle.

Months clean, she made grand gestures. Zoe showed pictures of her weapons on the steps. Her phone. I scrolled through witnessing gunmental. Someone tattooed with a sort of fortress up the forearm, asked after their cleaning. "Oils, rags. Stinks but keeps for showings." The bronze-clay mug slipped a bit and coffee shot steam drops at her open toes. Zoe and I had come into AA together. Hospitalized on respective male/female wards in the same treatment center, we'd seen each other a bit while clearing heads; and thus when running into one another at local meetings, we'd got on a bit. She was close to friends of mine with whom I'd swallowed drugs. I'd seen her on the night she apparently acquired an animal that pridefully rivaled her firearms. A snake, capable of constriction but I'm uncertain of its species beyond this. The fortressed gentleman had questioned her weeks prior about Dennis. "Snakes are the only animals that can fuck themselves. Dennis meets the criteria is all. One night piss drunk I'd gone car to car with what now seem like strangers. I'm uncertain who was with me. Henry says he saw me plopped on the couch at one point at somebody's place, but you can't believe what Henry says. I'd recognized an ex. This big-chested doofus. Someone even after, after you're going around apologizing? I left it. Anyway, strangers had asked for drugs of a kind, and somehow I'd put things together and I wind up at this place I mentioned. I enter, their money pressed against my nicked palms. I howl a bit. You know, I'm always howling on entering even now. So I go upstairs with somesuch, and big-chested doofus is there imbibing, whatever. Upstairs room and on the table is a smear of pharmaceuticals, choices. In the corner of it's a terrarium like? There's Dennis, and so he eyes me up a bit and I'm feeling touched, appreciated. I give money for drugs and am returned something that seems apt and so I wander off. In the car the strangers must've harassed me about the ineptitude of whatever I'd handed off, and so I'm sent pissdrunk back in to return either with compensation or restitution, drugs or money. I enter, I'm howling still. I make a show of it. Then something changes, a notion. Some anxiety jets up and I know what's certain: *their animal does not belong*. So I playfully like, take the snake from its terrarium upstairs, and I'm waving it about, and people are either scared or grossed out or shocked, and so I go. I leave. I'd grabbed some money I think, or dope, not sure, and thrown it to the strangers maybe. All I know is on waking I've got cut hands and this animal plopped in a hamper making sounds."

(The room seems just on edge and Henry's entrance does no good, he's pulled people from the rooms before and driven them to drink or use, he's had bad problems with a lack of confidence in certain principles perhaps, people shuffle around him and note his wounds and stench and a friend approaches Henry, they discuss Zoe's state, later Henry intones) "These therapists'll have your guts. It's enough sometimes to make you want to scream. I've tried time and again to be just what I ought but seldom find the comfort I find amid you all. Now you all might not like me much. Now you all might not want me here, but that's the problem for just us both. I need to be here, and we, we seem to need each other bad." (On meeting's end Henry stays around communicating with M. and several others later than usual, a window is opened and cigarettes are lit inside and the room seems barren as a church as they all avoid the temptation to find a stool, apologies end over end and the room's woodpaneling seems to spread against their talk, the lot of them occasionally rambling against the night, occasionally sitting there sipping coffee and smoking hard as ends are blotted out on the floor's concrete)

We know to take care of God him by the determination of our will and our own lives. We know that when he spoke to us through him even great efforts through prayer and meditation to understand the conscious contact with God, the strength of will to improve can enact this. To acknowledge arms at God and others is the exact nature of our failure. We have fully prepared to remove all the shortcomings of the character of God. We had our lives no longer, we were alcohol in content and deed. Start to believe that more force than they restore the spirit of our world. We know to take care of God him by the determination of our will and our lives. Do not worry about the moral resolution to him. To acknowledge God and others will be the exact nature of our failure. We have fully prepared to remove all the shortcomings of the character of God. Humbly asking him to remove our fear, our bodies. We harm no person on the list, we are ready to make all of us one. If you are unable to make rewards such as it is, so if you do not injure people, or others; offer funding. Put your personal inventory and when we were wrong, detect it early. We know that when he spoke to us through him even efforts through prayer and meditation to understand this conscious contact with God, the strength of will to improve can do that. The result is our next step to carry this message to alcoholics and those principles in our work had to apply for spiritual awakenings. It continues, immediately noting the individual asset, if we are wrong. Humbly ask God to eat alive our funding. Death disadvantage asked God (of our understanding). We harm everyone on our list, we want to reward them. The moral resolution and our own financial anxieties. Offer funding.

We'd all basically heard Zoe's account of matters previous. I'd likely heard it more than her recovery story, her origins. Dennis was something, I don't know. But shortly fortress had scrolled enough to find a strange bit of imagery with guns and snake and Zoe alike; my eyes they rolled. One weekend Zoe'd left for family concerns. Whenever she left she'd always ask after a few of us about Dennis's care. That particular time I'd opted, and experienced the sort of strangeness she seemed to see in him. The snake itself bore interest. I'm uneducated by and large regarding animals, but often just staring I find you'll understand just as well as poring over Darwin. An associative exercise, then. A poring into one's own history toward understanding subjectively what things do. I stared at first and sat deep in the couch while thinking. I thought of Alice Cooper. I thought of the animal eating its own tail. I thought of massive snakes attacking explorers. I thought of Eden. A snake is an anti-pet, I thought. Zoe didn't keep it around as a reminder. Zoe didn't keep a snake in her apartment to pet its skins. Zoe perhaps kept this snake because it worked contrary to any notion of pet-keeping we'd established as a people. She'd once attempted to talk to me of weapons, which might be why I think the way I do about it all. Zoe loved to talk of seas of things but weapons, Dennis, and her adherence to recovery loomed large above all smalltalk. It was this relationship to violence she established that drove my thinking. She kept a minor arsenal not because it protected her, not because her father'd kept them, not because they'd been handed down. She hadn't even kept guns prior to sobering up. She'd begun with one purchase after enduring trauma, and this slowly unfolded to the set she loved to show. She'd participate in these showings, but it wasn't that that kept her going either. She told me in the abstract about her fondness for contained aggression. The notion of holding something that all told desires death, and what to make of it. She'd talk about extremes like this with anyone she'd met in meetings. She'd admit to strange things like keeping tack in her foot during a job interview because without it anxiety was too great. She'd told me about abusive boyfriends past and rotten scenarios she'd lived through and often it was a marvel she'd stayed clean. I don't know how anybody stays clean. I don't know if anybody stays clean.

"Anybody here knows me. I'm Clyde, grateful recovering addict and alcoholic. (—*Hi Clyde*. Respectful banter emanates, laughter) "Here tonight to introduce one of my favorite souls you'll find in these plastic chairs. He's a hero of mine, a sponsee who's met and bested my every expectation of him. I'm proud to say that tonight lines up with the anniversary of an accident the likes of which doctors said Henry'd never recover from. His brain shut down that night and he wrapped his car around a pole not one block from a high school. Henry faced death, as most of you here tonight can ID, attest, and understand. Henry has wallowed in the marrow of this disease more than just about anyone I can name and he damn near lost it. Now I won't tell it all, but I want to commend you brother, for what you done and will do, these walls and outside. I'm proud to introduce Mr. Henry the Younger, and I hope you'll heed his say." (Affirmation circulates, a small wicker basket lined in red/white-checkered fabric is spread at the evening's bathetic low, mumbles and infrequent texting throughout the crowd regarding sex, last minute groceries, other more glaring matters, the room sits awful as Henry ascends, is handed his chip) "Hello, my name's Henry, and I'm an alcoholic." (—Hi Henry, suspended breath, anticipation) "Now I won't stand here and continue in Clyde's line if that's alright. I'm grateful to Clyde in more ways I know how to say but I've never been prideful in this rooms. Now I see new faces here tonight just like old. I see potential and a lot of damned heartache out there too. What I want to talk to you about then isn't tied to all that praise. What I'd like to do here tonight is share, confess, honest and see what comes. Last week I sat as fellows told on themselves for minor matters.

Admitted to not calling sponsors, not checking in and the like. Now I'll be honest with you I heard that and I lost nerve. I remembered the first meeting I sat in. Wednesday nights chaired by Clyde over at the hospital where my head'd been stitched up. I remember that room fulla sorry, smelly, penitent men and women all engaged in multiple sorts of recovery. Men and women so far gone they had to leave early for Methadone, Suboxone, Wellbutrin for smokes or smokes for not. I remembered that meeting and a pall shot through me. Pall's a word I tie to my daddy. He worked a funeral home all his life and he'd talk about a sort of veil, not black but maybe fleshtone, a pall he saw cast over life after all that. My daddy was big on poor man's PCP they call it now. He'd drink embalming fluid, dip cigars in it and sit down alongside corpses for hours too long until my mother'd come rouse him. I thought, now I think, that pall wavers just too much in degree. I see stories in newspapers about death panels and death squads and outbreaks of AIDS amid the broke third world, I think over us and what we make of our tragedy and wonder hard about what ought to be recalibrated. I've talked with oldtimers in here plenty about this sort of thing. Often it's said things have worked and will continue to. I don't suppose I disagree but I think on those moments, degrees of severity in the human condition. Civilizations where no word for war exists, no word for suicide. Makes you wonder at what we're doing here. Might make you sick or confused. I think on that more just now than much else, more than all the slips and missed calls and shirked behaviors. I wonder at the global conditions of my sobriety and I'm sorry to tell I have no answer for you, only more questions. If I'm truly honest that's the best I could offer you tonight. Only questions, no answers, and that's the draw of these rooms as it happens. In a number of months I'll have not drunk for roughly two years. Although I'm often hesitant to make head or tail of these matters, a sort of reflection nonetheless seems apt. For years one and two, and bits of change between then and now, I'd attend meetings, NA or AA, or meet with a counselor specialized in issues related to addiction. I'm not sure whether that was misguided, considering I'd decided in my third or fourth month of treatment that alternatives to AA or NA or standard means of sobriety-recovery simply didn't connect well with my thinking, but this was my approach those early months. I tend to obsess over things, big and small, it's just something I've always done. Those early months, then, I had to learn to experience joy, honestly experience it. I had to learn to smile at the world, and not turn away and wince like I'd done. Those early months, and still today, the past has been an enemy of mine. The past might be an enemy for every addict, every person. You've got to remind yourself in the early days to let certain things go. To forgive yourself. To try and live in the present. When people say 'move on' they aren't talking about looking into the future. The future's just as bad as the past for us. When people say 'move on' they mean that for once, for any length of time you can manage, you should appreciate the moment, settle yourself and know that for all the fuckups, and all the crimes and all the hurt you've strewn behind you, things aren't so bad as all that. They mean living in the present moment. They mean welcoming the day. Those first months, then, I needed to reimagine a world where I wasn't a miserable bastard. I needed to conceive of a world where I wasn't a criminal on the run. I needed to conceive of a life a bit absurd, a bit strange, but manageable. Even the worst of us, and believe me I've been one of the worst, and I've seen the worst, has something to redeem themselves, has something to hold onto every day. Those first months, then, I thought on the past, I thought on my father, and I tried to make a new world in my head. I likely failed. I fail every day. That's the most useful thing I could tell you here tonight though. We wake up, and we try, and we fail, and it's alright."

Of late, and for several years since first reading it, you think of Robert Stone's *Children of Light*. Lowry-ish drunks by the sea and schizophrenia. Attempting to reaffirm the notion that you no longer drink or take drugs recreationally, without the earmarks of an overall ideology or worldview to bolster up your abstinence. This is not a plea. Nor a declaration of suffering. Rather an attempt to suss out the possibility of living without the perspectival logic of an AA, an NA, a Rational Recovery, whatever. Your grandmother seemed quite comforted by calling herself an addict, an alcoholic. It soothed her to be named. *Children of Light*, then, functions simultaneously as a pat on the back when you've found yourself watching more television than sleeping on a daily/nightly basis—an O.K., it's not good but don't off yourself just yet—and further affirmation of the necessity of ritual in the lived days of a human animal in the twenty-first century. You think the same way of Exley, late in life, sitting on a couch with a jug of vodka and a container of ice cream. You think the same way of everyone. They're all there to pull you from yourself. To bring you outside of yourself. It's all you want. You want to be someone different, someone else. You want to be an image. You try things on. You put on possibilities. Read a bit and decide your fate. Decide your face. Sit in the cold and warm yourself with sleeping pills. Admittedly all seemed tempted to sip at black bile, the humors are amiss, blood requires letting. These were people dripped in stupor. It was time to sleep. Halls of dull glances, chemicals, chemicals. Swill at Byron's seed you're men as dogs. Barflies, Socratic. A poison, a little death, a hint perhaps to reach deep black. You think of literature and you think of tradition and you think of neglect and the walls and the walls and what walls. A reminder to live each day as if tomorrow you might be locked away forever. A reminder to the world that you're still breathing. A reminder to those lost that their memory holds. The days persist and they do not wait for you to figure anything out. The moments stretch and warp into a life and it needs tending. The addict is a person, the alcoholic is a person. The person is an animal. The animal is alone. Living is impossible, and yet. We tell ourselves stories, then, and try to rest. Your eyes are open.

Admitting—*I am your buddy. Today you'll meet your counselor, Becky. You will develop feelings for Becky. This is called* **transference**—*often more severe with us drunks. You will meet a handful of techs. Techs are sort of daily counselors, lesser a bit but O so relatable. J——, a large fellow of Islamic bearing, smokes two packs of Marlboros a day. He will become your favorite. He's my favorite. There's D—He's constantly taking in tobacco. Constantly. You will cry in front of him. You will spend your first seventy-two hours on the MSU, here with nurses, in case of withdrawal. You seem O.K. Are you O.K.? Court-ordered? Nutty parents? What? Did you bring cigarettes? Good. We've yet to go smoke-free. This week the leader of the unit is Michael. Michael was voted the leader by each of us and next week it will be somebody new. Tonight we'll go to the Y. You'll come along to the Y but then you'll have to head down here for bed. It's strange at first but then you get used to it. Gradually, suddenly. I'm on anxiety meds. I'm on depression meds. I love The Sopranos. I get out in a couple weeks. I'll get out of here right while you're settling in. There are classes to quit smoking. There are options to go to school here. There are ways of joining in. It's a good place. I came here from jail. Most of us came here from places that were awful. This place isn't so bad. Tonight we'll go to the Y.*

I sensed the danger, and discovered traces all around of her entangling herself in troubles. Dennis slept next to her. Zoe swore to being a light sleeper. I felt afraid when first she'd told me this. We'd sat in a diner with *Blue* in the title with another long-necked fellow who'd worked as a mechanic. All this settling down. My sense that everyone in those rooms had given in, and then she ups and admits. I'd been eating chicken-fried steak and eggs. Coffee, we'd drunk gallons of coffee in knowing one another. The long-necked man and I had discussed Ayn Rand. I'd felt embittered about the God question in those rooms and thus sought out alternatives, read the Russian émigré and found a sense I admired. I'd deliver subs during the day and listen to a recording of an actor named Edward Herrmann reading from *Atlas Shrugged* and then when long-neck grimaced at her works I'd attempted and failed at justifying anything. Human selfishness, I've since come to appreciate, is not a philosophy so much as a justification for immorality. We're born selfish enough, is all, but most teenagers and twenty year olds are dumb. I sat there defending a bit and Zoe I guess needing to change the pace of talk asked after our families. Shortly thereafter, as was her way, she'd coiled back to her parents, the absence of significant others, and Dennis, and out it came that the two would bed together. I understood people like Zoe better than anybody in meetings. They needed a sort of visceral escape in life and something that put them outside the daily concerns of us. People who misunderstood them called them terminally unique. In treatment people pierced all sorts of things. People cut. People hated themselves. People railed their meds. They needed something to connect them. Most wind up taking some sort of extreme martial art or joining a violent religious tradition. I understood it and I wanted to share myself with them. I was there for people like them I guess. I was part of it. I wanted to be guilty too. I wanted to inquire and have her say it out loud but I didn't need to. I was just as fucked up and pathetic. I didn't ask it but I might've just as well. She mumbled and shied away and showed us ever more pictures from her phone. The light in there was terrible and we'd stumbled somewhere beyond a human comfort. I understood this need to see oneself as vulnerable, as beyond vulnerable, as torn, as split by something, as ripped in half. I knew this feeling, I'd wanted it. I'd sit in the bathroom late with the lights off and drag knives over me. I'd done every drug suicidally. I'd drunk suicidally. I'd stolen and committed crimes and persisted in doing so even for a time after getting clean and I fucked up and fucked up and wanted that open sort of living. Zoe wanted an open sort of living. Zoe wanted her life to register. Zoe wanted her life to mark this earth, etch into it. I understood it. I understood it and nothing surprises me anymore.

Bill W. and the history of these meetings between men who'd made an ugly mess of their lives and persistent sexism still and the narrative biased toward the father and the image of Christ above our heads. The bloated American Christ. All the sad twentieth century misogynists. Jackson Pollock careening in a car too drunk to think. Still the rooms tend to reek of this. The narratives are simplified. Perhaps it's necessary. Perhaps the drugs are too impossible to quit without. What can be forgiven. What does progress look like. This tradition of abusive monsters redeeming themselves through art. This history of vile behavior. The assumption any of it's necessary for the work. The assumption any of it does anything but destroy. The impossibility of movement. A plague destroying cities. Heroin. *Heroin.* Watch your life become a series of dirty injections and scabs. Watch your life. Watch your happiness dwindle. Watch the chemicals in your head begin to rebel. *My brain wants me dead. My body wants me dead. My history wants me dead. My lineage wants me dead. I want me dead.* It all rings out. Calls to strangers in small smelly rooms and apologies given to nobody at all for our living and the need for some escape.

"Now what I do is drink coffee and bet. I know they meet here too the G.A.s but it's enough already one thing at a time. One day they say. I try. I haven't seen my daughter since I was put up. Her father's good. Real together. I haven't seen her in eight months. I'm grateful though in what ways make sense to me. Sick to death of yall's ugly mugs but here we are. My brother called me a liar the other night. Believe that? I stay with him and his and I did my step four crying my damn eyes out in his living room with Ella here and he saw that pain but the other night his car's low on gas he accuses me. I say, ask her, ask your kids. Damn kid looks more stoned than I ever was wearing hoops through every hole and bigol stretched out ears. Feral little shit. I said no, I did nothing and you can't accuse me this way. I am clean. Still haven't returned. He calls and his wife calls and they apologize but I'd rather just stay at Sojourner's House you want the truth. No judgment no nothing. City of damn hypocrite confused babies. I can only take just so much. My mother was a drunk. My father was a drunk. My cousins all got the disease. We all commune over the dead those of us who've stayed quit. The rest hate us, they detest us. My brother mostly hates me I figure. I don't mind. I don't want to live on someone's couch. I don't know where I want to live. I don't want to be a charity case. I'd like to be a counselor. All of us wind up becoming counselors. Only thing we know how to do is talk to fuckups like us after we get clean. Only thing we can do is maintain and keep one another near. My brother, though. I can't take this liar business. I can't be called a liar after everything. I was a liar. I might still be a liar. How can someone know? Whatever. He doesn't know. He can accuse all he wants.

His family can hate me. I don't care. I just need the dirty damn couch until I save enough for a first month and deposit. I can't wait to leave. Hurts being called bad things after we come here. We fuck up. We scorch the earth of our family lives. We ruin friendships. We ruin marriages. We cheat. We lie. We steal. We run away. We escape. We chase a feeling. We step on anyone who gets in our way. But if we leave it, if we hang it up. What then? Can't we be left to move on? Can't we be free?" (Ella walks over for a hug, the share passes on to an ex-football player who sells used cars who hasn't drunk in twenty-five years but comes here every single day no matter what, coffee is circulated and numbers are exchanged, the cold leaks in)

Lives difficult to manage. We gave, were stronger than gambling. It continues, immediately recognized the individuals' assent, if we were wrong. We were hellish, manage our lives. We are aware that this or they have an impact on the family/dysfunction/other. Start believing that more force than they can restore the spirit of our own. That if it is humbly and proposes it, nor you. Or at least not to me, it is short shrift. Those who believe that the restoration of health to arm themselves with more. I humbly ask our efforts' defects. For all he had injured numbered, and there were all will do. We understood that the teaching of prayer and meditation with God, praying only looking for a better awareness of the power of God in us and it will be. I cannot be parsed with to relate to what others will do. O keep my soul, and my honor, I stand at a safe remove within the accompanying, and I will stay within the venom of the gods. It belongs to I, as well as traffickers in precious cloths of yarn convictions, direct us to God our God of the word, and to contribute to constructive, generous power. Mutt. Once I woke up as I was, with my own, both in the actions of the gods, and with the word, and I will that they are healthy, and so with the honor of future happiness. Such is to be satisfactory, except when this would be, or harm your elders. Generous power hospitality. Let them be confounded all the gods, the quality of our offering and the other that we should be chosen. Generous power of faith.

"I once returned home from a boy's place and caught an inkling, and so took a handful of however many Wellbutrin in attempts to make some push. I spent the night discussing holes with businessmen from wherever until they realized I wasn't close to meeting them for plasticky, blooded closeness. I also did more straightforward things, drank or used amphetamines with older persons, took cocaine a number of times and woke up oddly wounded; but given my aforesaid gutful approach to chemical intake, there was often no rhyme or reason to my use. If there were drug or drink apparent and I might ingest them with what money I had or no fear of trouble should I steal them, I would then ingest them. With time this led to mild legal trouble, time spent in kiddie jails and the like, and my resignation to the prospect of dying at twenty-one without much in the way of an emotional tug. It wasn't tragic, per se, and there are countless accounts of chemical abjection more pressing, but it occurred, became mythed, and confidence arose of my addictive/alcoholic head, and thus some means of staying quit seemed desirable. The car accident accelerated matters, as I remembered exactly none of it, and had so thoroughly destroyed my car and self as to need recovery for months and assistance still today. I'm grateful to my sponsor and to Zoe for all their help in this regard. I don't know how anybody manages to stay clean, but all I can do is try to keep at it. For me, what I do, I'm unsure. Certainties: I take a low dose of Fluoxetine, Buspirone (causes horniness, is a problem) each day. I walk, I talk to myself. I listen to loud things. I write loud things down. I watch television, enormous amounts of television. I read things, minor things, things of the addictive state. Poe and Burroughs and

Shulamith Firestone and Malcolm Lowry and minds galore in fluid. The AA meeting itself a reading. A place to chat. A salon. A group of citizens of likened plight. Find myself a friend or two with whom to gripe at my status on this rock. Take comfort rather than concern from long conversations with my pet. Assert my discomfort in my skin and masturbate frequently. Find out things and forget them and become someone I don't recognize. Get a library card, check out materials, don't watch or read them and return them in months when it's freezing cold. These are my methods." (Room is given over to laughter and embrace, Henry is greeted with long hugs from Clyde and Zoe and dessert is spread around the room and things feel content, whole)

Step 3 Prompt: Find your Higher Power Through Desire: Compose a list of anything you can imagine wanting. Find your God (as you understand Him) thus. Start by saying "I want" and see what comes. Repeat this exercise until you've come upon a list that feels genuine. Share it.

I WANT DEATH. I WANT ABJECTION. I WANT SORROW. I WANT PILLS. I WANT WHINING. I WANT CONSTRUCTION SITES. I WANT FORGERY. I WANT ORSON WELLES. I WANT NIGHTMARES. I WANT SLEEP. I WANT FATNESS. I WANT EVERY DOG. I WANT FAT SKIN. I WANT EVERY DOG. I WANT TO DIE FOR YOU. I WANT TO WATCH ME DIE. I WANT TO BECOME IMPALED. I WANT TO DRINK. I WANT TO DRINK. I WANT TO DRINK. I WANT TO SWALLOW PILLS. I WANT TO SWALLOW STOLEN PILLS. I WANT TO BREAK INTO YOUR HOME AND SWALLOW YOUR PILLS. I WANT TO SEE YOU SLEEPING. I WANT TO WAIT AND SEE. I WANT TO WATCH YOU WEARY.

She'd called it a form of worship, she'd whispered it gasping terrified into the phone imploring I'd come. A ritual. She'd fucked up. It wasn't as severe as it seemed, she insisted. It made sense, she insisted. I worked up some nerve so early in the day and left home to go and check on Zoe's condition. To molt she'd said. I saw her suicidal. She'd wanted to molt a bit, to experience something between species. I'd noticed caverns of snakeskin that looked as if knives had dragged dull and rusted across its shine. Some sort of mucus emanated, spilled outward. She'd cut herself sufficient along the ribs to leak, blood glistened along her sides. The both in a pathetic roll of fleshbits on the carpet and stuck fragments of fabric lined their cuts as she attempted to explain. Tears welled from her eyes and she could barely speak without adrenaline closing her throat. I listened and I closed my eyes. I knelt alongside the two and tried to make decisions. The snake grew irritable and slung its form in various directions attempting to flee. She'd held it between her legs and slit their skins in equal length, she insisted. I watched and a note of madness held the scene, bits of iron or copper wafted up from their openings. A tragedy, a catastrophe, she insisted. Dennis seemed to encourage her desire to molt and let things go, she'd taken something and the room had bloomed to surgery, welcomed it. My caution wasn't over their survival, neither seemed on the edge of death. Really her cuts looked like scarification, intentional and sterile. My caution was over explanations, ways of making sense and putting the incoherent into start and finish. I walked into her kitchen and took off my boots. I felt the skin of my feet on tile on removing socks and tried to calm myself, to ease my heart from my throat, a method in a sort of biofeedback my mother'd shared. I stood there as they made simple animal clicks and inhalations on the floor and heard as rolls led to pulled carpet and inserted bandages. They'd looked filled with asbestos, the carpet cheap and institutional. I wondered what she took and then didn't at all; things I guess transcended. Cells aligned or synapses and I knew well what to do. My hands seemed to sweat blood. I grabbed sheets and sponges, tapes and clean-looking fabrics from where they hung. I grabbed a cup and warmed its water. I breathed in through my nose and tried to grimace. On entering the room again I registered the smell. Notes of bleach compounded the iron and copper and burnt dogends of chemicals. Blackened bulbs on table and bottle of clear smeary booze or cough medicine cupped and howling. I fell by her side and began to clean their wounds. I dragged wetted fabric against and pulled carpet away as it stuck with small tugs and scabbing pulling back. I removed and cleansed, watched the strange shapes Dennis took under the pressure, his gasping toward violence against my forearms. Zoe winced and seemed to sleep her head flat back against the ground as Dennis inched his cheek to temple. They were cohering again, endless. I felt an ancient nausea then, ritualistic and bound up in religious pornography. I held her side against me to tighten the fabric and create a wrapping. She coiled then and Dennis seemed to mimic and I undid lengths of tape and pressed it to her. To him I did same taking cracked bloody breaths against the oncoming sun and when it overwhelmed I fell to floor myself and held her head against my chest. She tried to speak, to clarify, to qualify against what she imagined were my ideas. I felt it but discouraged it still. I didn't need explanation. We'd moved beyond wording, seen a limit and pushed beyond it what we could and I was guilty. I held her head until she seemed to calm and before leaving I bagged up what chemicals I saw and turned on her television. I find myself doing this often. I felt confident she wouldn't pass but nothing like certainty.

You watch them become dwindled to the point of falling apart, then steal their valuables to pawn. These are not good lives. These are not lives well-spent. Bask a bit beneath the glow of poppies and glaze. You are dying. You can feel it clear as day. If it isn't this then any number of affectations resultant will devour you. Ode to the friend who did not save my life. Your skin is marked and rotting. Your arms are pocked and splitting. A night in jail. A light above your head that won't go out, its sound. A night becomes a month. A blur of violence around you. You're mailed books brand new from stores by your father who's tired of hearing you're right on the edge of death. It isn't possible to live knowing someone you love is about to die. You are perpetually about to die and the world will watch you make this mistake over and over and over again. You've never been violent. A sinking feeling as the last days seem to be upon you. A guilt-ridden upbringing leaves you wondering at hells. You think of your carriage across the sea to a life of torture. You think of Bas Jan Ader floating alone and scared and unable to scream. You wonder about that final ride. You wonder about the man who'll take you and whether you'll be left with any pennies on your eyes to make your way. It is a deathly business. You've seen people nights and woken up to smell their corpses.

You've watched films late into the night with lovers to wake up to the heaving silence of their not-breath. You deserve it, you think. You should be tortured end over end, burnt on spits and fed to emaciated children. You weep for a kind of dying. Times had been simpler living in the city and taking turns each day visiting doctors and complaining of something and vomiting or screaming out or asking for some water something to ease the throat and then stealing the prescription pad and running and running out of there as fast as you could and selling what you could and ordering drugs across the city and picking them up together. Times had been simpler before injecting before encountering the risk encountering the sting and the feeling of sleep warming through your skull and welcoming it and falling to sleep only to realize after months you'd been infected. You'd lived in fear of being caught for stealing and now lived in fear of rotting some morning on the porch of some stranger and spreading your disease. One day you pick up a test kit with stolen money from Walgreens and take it in a tunnel nearby a light coating of snow on the ground. The test kit says to swab your cheek you do so and wait and sit there and an animal approaches and you hiss. The test confirms what you've known instinctively and thus your solitude and thus your slow acceptance of this starved death.

(Asked for readiness) "So when I came in I think I'd been withdrawing kinda hard for maybe three days? I got put on Suboxone and suddenly I'm sat down alone in the caf with a cup of coffee and some saltines and they lay out the MMPI in front of me. I stared at it for like hours trying to find a way in. I haven't taken tests or anything since I was in high school and they had those sheets? With the bubbles you fill in? Have you ever been asked if you liked playing with mud and had to respond in bubble-form? It was ridiculous. I wanted to die. I sat there staring but eventually Kimmy walks by and Kimmy's my roommate and like my best friend in here and she goes *I LOVE DIGGING FOR WORMS!* and I just died. We both laughed for like an hour. I've seriously never laughed that hard I mean my hips hurt! But so that was like the start, I think? I didn't see this place as so negative maybe after? I had some hope. And now after twenty-eight days coming here, I guess I mean yea I do feel ready. I'm from this town so everybody knows that if you drink a bit you'll wind up here you know? You lose friends in high school everyone says but suddenly you get reacquainted at meetings when you're thirty or whatever. I'm still young I guess but I can't fuck up anymore. Sometimes I do think about pot maybe, you know? But I never really had a problem with pot so we'll see. Right now I just can't wait to find some work and get out of my parents' place. Seriously. I cannot wait."

Works if you work it. There's no chemical solution to a spiritual problem. While you're in here, your addiction is pissed off in the parking lot doing push-ups. One day at a time. K.I.S.S. Keep It Simple Stupid. Your best thinking got you here. First the drunk takes a drink, then the drink takes a drink, then the drink takes you. By the grace of my higher power and the fellowship and community of my home group I'm now X months clean, X years clean. I was sober but not in recovery. I was white-knuckling. I was a dry drunk. I slipped. I relapsed. I had to go back out there. I needed to do more research. These walls. Grant me the serenity to accept the things I cannot change, the courage to change the things I can and the wisdom to know the difference. God help me. Thy will not mine be done. Principles before personalities. Eric Clapton. Reginald "Bubbles" Cousins. Johnny Cash. Sid Vicious. Nancy Spungen. William Seward Burroughs II. Steal boat to row across the lake at Center City for booze. Sell your skin for a fix. Temperance. Tee-totalers. Bill W. and tumblers of gin. Bill W. and LSD 25. Bill and Dr. Bob meet Carl Jung and navel gaze. Akron. Promises. Betty Ford. Hazel's Den. Postwar wifebeaters. Just for today. Work your program. Work the steps. Trust in your higher power. Stinkin' thinkin'. Addict behavior. I've got the disease. The disease concept. Turn it over. Hit a meeting. Donate what you can. State-funded twelve-step rehabilitation. Recovery monopolies. Rational Recovery. Healthy realization. Cognitive Behavioral Therapy. Needles. Just this old guitar and an empty bottle of booze. God is nice. AODA. Jail time or drug treatment. Self-sufficient. Church and state and the land of ten thousand treatment centers. Rehab conventions. Sober hookups. Sober dating apps. Sober dances. Sober dormrooms. A culture. Mea culpa. Intervention. Memoirs. Suffering. Faces. Neglected kids. Anxiety hangover. Antidepressants. Serotonin reuptake inhibitors. MAO inhibitors. Prozac nation. Frederick Exley. Malcolm Lowry's strangled wife. Malcolm Lowry's Mexico. Winston Churchill drank a glass of brandy with breakfast. Chemicals. Languages. Who you see here what you hear here when you leave here let it stay here. Raymond Carver pre and post. A wine bottle broken over the head of his wife. Kids neglected and entire lives neglected and excuses. Excuses. Excuses. Every musician's emaciated trials. Hubert Selby Junior. Christopher Moltisanti. Barrels of solutions. Cult rituals. Annual chips. My mother had it. Abraham Lincoln suffered clinical depression. The war on drugs. Nancy Reagan. Life is suffering. A million little pieces. Just stop. Just say no. Turn your will and your life over. Turn it over. Let go and let God. We will not regret the past nor wish to shut the door on it. Visiting prisons. Read your Big Book. Do the work. Pay attention. Listen to the old-timers. Works if you work it.

There wasn't a rationale behind my leaving, but the resultant wave of inhumanity I felt and sprawling guilt cut clear as day as it hung down and I couldn't stop walking until I'd seen water; was then submerged. I would return after I told myself. I would return and ease my guilt, buy her breakfast, make everything O.K. I would return. I walked into the guts of a nearby pond and buried my head in darkness for what time I could. I felt the mud against my hands and sharpnesses of bottles against my fingertips and palms. I closed and opened my eyes welcoming dirt and felt them redden or vessels pop and looked up to see the sun blotted against gray cloudcover and suddenly smelled the pox of that room. I felt the intake of air and watered lung so rose to short hacking bloodbits into mud. I felt unsure just where I was and noted families walking by in morning with strollered children. I felt the pressure to die and slapped my head wet against a near rock. I was largely unobserved and continued guilt held my guts. I lay on my back with slight bleeding in head to watch the sky unravel. The next day's evening I'd taken Zoe to a meeting and we'd talked over matters, sobriety, whatever. Extremes. I told her I'd once attempted to eat a massive book. I told her I knew someone who'd cut their cock each night. I told her that there was no right way of living. I told her she might need medicine. I told her I understood why she'd done it.

This, if anything at all from all that muck and dross bears interest still years later; is all that interests you. It interests you because once you read a piece on an individual hopelessly addicted, and his eventual sobriety on taking a particular cocktail of non-high-inducing muscle relaxers—or somesuch—and the paucity you'd read elsewhere of such cases. Sobriety, recovery, addiction, depression, these are largely literary things. The memoir in each of these four maladies is an abundant field, and no small number of pens have either drunk or drugged to get word writ well, or cleaned up and found a sudden desire to piss and bleed atop some typewriter howling woe-is-they. This isn't merely for the professorial cough-syrup suckler, however, as that is boring. This is just a small declaration, perhaps, or somesuch leaning toward graffitied scrawls on Club 12/AA recovery hall doors.

Making a searching and fearless moral inventory: fell asleep at wheel, killed Myra's cat, dropped child in anger on bed, possibly hurt people while drunk and don't remember, possibly took advantage of people or was violent while on drugs or drunk and don't remember, possibly a vile pig horrible person rapist murderer and don't remember anger at wife anger at kids anger at dog anger at neighbors anger at boss anger at family anger at friends anger at not drinking anger at the thought of drinking anger at legalization of weed anger at people misunderstanding anger at television anger at lack of television called sister a "vapid whore", drunk and on handful of sleeping pills at brother's graduation, stole neighbor's drugs, stole other neighbor's drugs, stole other neighbor's drugs, went into friend's medicine chest, stole drugs, stole money, stole checks, stole mom's jewelry (pawned, can buy some pieces back w/in 6 mos) moral by whose standard? mine? My higher power is Satan. General Patton. John Henry. I FUCKED UP!!! Forgive me daddy, forgive me mommy, forgive me friend, all I do is make mistakes moral by my standards. Mural. I neglected wife and kids. I'm a cliche I'm a cliche I'm a cliché I'm a cliché I'm a cliché -my mother's brother's father's cousin touched me, was an addict. Nobody loves me. Now all I do is watch television. I watch television about addiction. My life is a useless feedback loop of lies and excess. Hate this world. Hate this tendency in me. Hate voice of me. Hate voice in head. Can't write it down. Can't put thoughts down. Steal from everyone. Steal from everywhere. Mistake every day another mistake. Hate this life.

I remember cooking for the floors of my halfway house. A Latin fellow named M—laughed on entering that I was playing Dean Martin. I'd laugh and sing. A recovering addict of methamphetamine with severe Autism would change to modern metal. He worked as a janitor at the Metrodome. I made pasta and set the table with significant flourish. I worked days carrying groceries to cars at Byerly's. I once walked home in the hot sun eating a rotisserie chicken. I made them dinner and like kids we played "Territorial Pissings" and buried our heads in couches.

1230 Brown Bag Meeting–Montessori School Downtown "I've held to the nuance of NA. Drugs are new, Pound's new. Chemicals adapt. Booze is stubborn, curmudgeonly, dejected. I was formerly an arborist. We'd drunk at sites and spent days laughing belly-up. Amphetamines came along like bats and made the days sublime. I was studied, learned a bit. I feel sick often. I don't know how to reconcile whatever it is I am at present with whatever it was I'd done to get me here. I know I've done some horrible things. I'm certain of it, as are various police departments surrounding Minneapolis. I don't feel bothered by that though. The courts, there's animosity. There's already a refutation when I walk in the door. They hate us, we hate them, that whole bit. NA I enjoy because it feels like we exist on the edge of something. I enjoy that. I enjoyed treatment when NA was embraced. There were LGBTQ groups tied with NA in my halfway house and my roommates and I were all kind of hoping for a more cutting-edge approach to recovery. We wore patches and ate nicotine jobs where we were forced to work and gritted our teeth through days in Minnesota summer while the towns drank and boated to quick deaths. Lot of things gone now that might've been. Whole careers gone now but if I'm honest I prefer the way things've gone. Worse-off souls than myself have made good even after accidental murder and I guess I take great comfort in knowing that."

She tended to articulate things quite too late. She wasn't confrontational, and welcomed up-to-date accounts of why she'd failed, only to later scream and tear hairs over what was said. Then she couldn't sleep. At first she'd lay and work over writing she'd begun and stopped toward a degree in Art's history. She'd written about whether it might be inferred from his engravings if Albrecht Dürer suffered from clinical depression, whether painting weren't a sort of drug. Similar theories existed for van Gogh, Dostoevsky. Their work created in a hypergraphic attempt to stave off misery, not unlike the drunk, not unlike the addict. This writing itself begun as a retort against a friend who'd opted she'd be better off taking natural remedies for melancholy and exercising than by what pills she'd seen. By then the friend had graduated and she nowhere closer to Albrecht's open head. This: at first. Then however she'd left her monograph and begun visual work of her own, enacting whole cities of skin with oilwork well into the day's light then leaving for walks and lecturing. Her work took walls, over time, and thus she'd paid for student space in a studio that slowly filled with worried takes. She'd become hypnotized by dark, was how she'd conveyed her state to you. There just seemed so much heft in death, absence, in spare takes on being. She'd attend defenses of graduating works and make puddles of spit on the ground in front of her while the rooms erupted in tears or claps. The world around her seemed heavily concerned with things that made her skin wince, and thus she'd wallow in that state poring over what she'd done, unable to flee the scene. Nothing worked, nothing was working. She'd left her studio work with a floor sopped in red and mumbled around a bodega for minutes until placing her face against the cool surface of glass and staring in. The room became accusatory, she couldn't do this. She grabbed what seemed a mealy red apple and relented, grabbed a bottle of wine and enacted the purchase process without wholly looking at the clerk. Wielding paper bag she hugged the brick and stepped along the street leaning so as to create an angled figure. Her head occasionally rubbed the stone and she felt bits of it trail off her hairs and clack softly against her calves. She walked thus until she came upon an entrance to a park, it wasn't quite day. Nothing made sense. Runners around, workers shuffling.

I WANT CAVES. I WANT TO GO TO HELL. I WANT TO ROT IN HELL. I WANT TO BE KICKED IN THE TEETH BY A TEXAN. I WANT TO BE KICKED DEAD. I WANT TO FEEL MY OWN DEATH. I WANT TO SWALLOW ANTIDEPRESSANTS. I WANT TO TAKE ANTIDEPRESSANTS. I WANT TO SEE THERAPISTS. I WANT TO PISS ON SIGMUND FREUD'S GRAVE. I WANT TO WATCH YOU CHANGING. I WANT TO HEAR YOU WEEPING. I WANT TO IMBIBE. I WANT TO SIT AT BARS AND SNEER. I WANT TO SMOKE. I WANT TO FEEL LIKE SMOKE. I WANT TO USE HEROIN. I WANT TO USE YOU. I WANT TO USE METHAMPHETAMINE AGAIN. I WANT YOU HERE. I WANT TO SLEEP WELL. I WANT TO SLEEP WELL. I WANT TO TAKE NARCOTICS. I WANT TO PRAY TO GOD. I WANT TO WITNESS GOD. I WANT TO SEE THE FIRST DAY OF LANGUAGE. I WANT TO SMELL MYSELF CORRODING. I WANT TO WHISPER WHERE I'M HIDDEN. I WANT TO READ THE LITERATURE. I WANT TO PRINT BROCHURES. I WANT TO SEE THINGS HAPPEN. I WANT TO WIN THE PRESIDENCY. I WANT TO KNOW EVERY WORD. I WANT TO SLEEP IN EVERY CAVE. I WANT TO WATCH A CITY BURN. I WANT TO KILL MYSELF.

(An order asserts itself and they are drawn into groups communicating about a range of things, commiserating over a range of concerns) "I worry over friendship. A concept, there is no concept, if there is a concept it is buried in his veins and if veins can run his have run to the ends of his hands just before the beginning of his fingers and there the end of any potential concept currently sits as he raps his fingers in sequence on the counter awaiting the return of the keys to his car that he will thus walk outside, start, and drive home where the beginning of other concepts will present themselves. Period. Tonight he'll scrape his veins for dogends, my brother. I've gone to Al-Anon, filled with voices. I've listened and tried to find sense, only found more language, more ways of defining something that puts more distance between us and it. Tonight my brother will likely OD for the nth time and I'll be somewhere sober and wholly aware that there's next to nothing I'll be able to do until he hits bottom, another concept. I use to stay close to him. I used to try and remain close even as our friends and family slowly left us by the wayside. I was convinced I needed to be there for him and to stop him. I've learned in here that's wrong, but I still fixate. I've learned in here that I'm supposed to let go, but I don't know how much. I never know how much. He's got friends, is all. He's got friends and it drives me mad to think about it. It all drives me mad to think about it. I am not him. I am not his addiction. I cannot be his addiction. I cannot be sober for him. All I can do is express myself, and make people aware, and try. It's not enough and I'm stuck thinking over concepts then. Useless useless work. I'm addicted to him, to his sense of things, to hope for him. It's hopeless. It's useless.

I'd do better with despair but still tomorrow I'll buy him lunch and hope while I hug him."

How are you sure since I've grown a bit, I've found myself staring at pretty much, I stare at men, women, cars, buildings, waitresses employees, from all walks of life, and the same goes for stuff like, and motionless. I cannot explain it, something about putting all my thoughts, all my urges to this person I do not have anything in common with the exception of our flesh, and with regard to the buildings, I like to imagine the origin, purpose, builders, people inside, all the perverse ways in which I had the it. Perfect exists. I said loudly into the night and anyone who would listen to me. I remember thinking the car on admissions psychotherapy my past. Thinking about the time when I was much younger and my mother happened to me. There was no day lying. We were both on the same page as this way interprets, but I still did not want to be there, I still wished there was some other way than this. So what'd you want to talk about bud buried my face with warm water, thinking about my dad all day finally led me to the hard times, times when he would say sentences to those like, why do you not get a job, or you've had it really easy in life, and I was just furious. I mean it was not like there were not times when I was obedient, not active, but it and my mother they forced me to quit, and into meetings of AA, and when I was young, they forced me to the hospital to talk about my depression and inevitably get me pills prescribed, and yet, a few days ago, he came out of left field with this anger toward me what he thinks I'm doing and I would be infuriated. When I finally got home blitzed, I drank a whole bottle of whiskey, took all the pills and sat smoking. Identification, I stumbled inside, having locked in the garage and the return of all the mothers of my possessions to the order, I did a good job of it that way. At this point, we go together we have one class together at the very end of our day here. We both had class last year together. That's the only thing I do not understand, you live in a place that's real, and full of corruption and repression, but at the same time your nights are as real as they are in fucking Zimbabwe, people here do not understand the country in which you live has little impact on day to day life surrounding. I mean look at us, we're just two young idiots, going down the street from a movie, get into our cars and drive home to eat a quick meal before we go to sleep. I mean some places are horrible. I stared out the window what should be crazy. But its truth only in the back of the hill someone created a building of this hospital. He tried to apologize and eventually he said to go back to my unit, but I did not care, or probably never respected my counselors a lot of life and was pretty lousy myself. So I just sat in the hall and did not think about anything.

TWO

"He seemed to himself acutely aware of everything."
—*Recovery*, John Berryman

Boys and girls surround a writer asking at his state. His hands are noted. His veiny hands gesture at the air and they feel they leave trailings of insight. Dust, an old man besotted with dust. Every wince and movement leaving a puff of intellect awaft and they cannot keep up. They'd gone to the Fitzgerald theater together and seen Wilde performed. This was their evening's seminar. He gestured seated within the living room smoking and the walls and wood made waves of emotive beacon. Long yawping phrases left his mug as a young undergraduate with child held his hand to help him through. He'd created a beheaded corpse of sorts with what he'd done. Pieces were released. People spoke. He began to see the literary enterprise bleed over to the drinker's enterprise and on to the recovery enterprise. A community of souls who wanted most to say exactly the right phrase leveling their guts. Le mot juste. The Dream Songs the Cantos and the Wasteland enter a tavern, Li

Po is serving tea. He was able to talk because he was able to lie. He was able to share himself with those around him without opening himself at all. He was able to run the water over his wrists at the hottest temperature in the bathroom without even wincing. He'd taken some sort of cure. He'd prayed himself into a corner of some cure. His hands were showing his pulse. He could've become addicted to anything then. He remembered watching TV sets in wards and being asked questioned by professionals and their white clothing and their Thorazine. He could read in there and often simply laid a copy of an English usage dictionary on his lap and read through every single thing. The work was apparent. The work was at hand. He was being rewarded. There were moments of praise. He lied through his teeth at these. He lied through his teeth at his wife and often forgot about those under his responsibility, his auspices. His shelf in his office featured volumes of the work and he stared at bottles of Bayer medications and ran his fingers through his beard. Hairs were falling out. His rooms were slowly invaded. His life was slowly invaded. His world was cracking at the seams and he couldn't remember every lie. He couldn't keep straight with himself and never could. The words came out disjointed, fragmented, odd.

Significant Other Pact #946 "I will not drink or consume pills for fun so long as I live. My mother intook a tall cup of scotch and two Valium for postpartum depression after nine kids and wound up intervened at fifty years old. She wept and we were coached to react. We failed in that respect and so wept. My father could not cope. I followed in her jagged footsteps. I don't want to keep following those footsteps. I want to be better. I need to be better. I want you to help me. I promise this won't happen again."

XXX "When I was nineteen years old in New York in 1987 I was beaten to near death by a group of misunderstanding teenagers outside a club who'd just seen Cro-Mags and took their lifestyle immensely seriously. I asked them, I asked for something. I asked for money, for dope. They laughed a bit and began to kick my skull with boots. This isn't bathos. I don't need pity for what they'd done. It just interests me looking back. I cleaned up and in meetings you see plenty of diehard straightedge kids but just then they'd gone to some other place of zealotry. They caved in my right eye a bit and if my head swells up at all I feel it push my eye outward and upward and can get a bit nauseated thus. I take Excedrin whose caffeine seems to help. I take caffeine in numerous forms and work at a small recovery center in Hoboken where not much changes. I remember being beaten not because I stopped right away. I remember the degrees. They had manifestos. I'd seen their shows. I'd admired Judge and various members of the bands away in prison I'd written them in fandom even before cleaning up just for the sake of what they'd made. I hung around in clubs. There was a militancy. I fell in love with their clothing. I tried to look like them. I tried to be these other people. I wanted to exist in their skins. I wanted to be consumed as they were. I let the music wash over me. I became involved by accident."

Louis Malle and Le Feu Follet. The Fire Within. Oslo August 31st. We are all addicted to the mythos of a romantic death. A life done well, made noble by dying, perhaps. You walk into an AA meeting with a paperbag atop your head and start to weep. Wake up. Make bed. Say prayers. Use bathroom. Write for a bit and wait until room check. Converse a bit with roommates. Retch a bit in light. Masturbate. Hide. Become anxious. Take medication in a line of slippered males. Smell the morning of the place. Enjoy one cigarette. Carry your crossword. Attend group therapy. Wish happy birthday to such-and-so. Think about life in a rainforest. Imagine a better world. Read a bit of poetry from your sister. *77 Dream Songs*. Become nauseated. Read some letters from your family. Write responses to your family. Think about your daughter. Think about animalistic urges. Take your noontime medication. Attend a meeting regarding smoking. Become aroused. Use the bathroom and masturbate in utter quiet. Return and stare at your counselor's khaki pants. Ask her about Wellbutrin's use in such matters. Remember going fishing. Think about Medicine Lake nearby and whether you should leave. Flee. You wonder over Jonathan. Former roommate decided to leave one night. You'd disabled your alarm so as to pass notes with female occupants above. Smoking cigarettes at night past lights out. You miss Jonathan. You want to feel complete and whole and you know pretty well this is not something you're going to feel shortly. The myth of the Dionysian artist, the drunk Faulkner, Lowry, Hemingway, Louisa May Alcott and opium. You suffer O so hard is how it's read. Bacchanals because creativity requires it. Eat yourself. You remember a story of Frederick Exley having dinner with some friends and sitting on the couch afterward (JOURNEYONADAVENPORT) with a pint of ice cream and a large bottle of vodka. Something childlike in that, an adult sort of teething. *Well, I watch television.* Indeed.

The air made her a bit nauseated as she slid against the grass and leaves to sit her tights on wet earth. She watched as people passed and pressed her teeth to the apple. The mealy red apple was disgusting. She sucked at it until it felt she'd removed all its liquid and then spat high up into the air so that its contents showered over her and mingled with the brick. She fed Swiss Army corkscrew into the wine and pulled between her legs and felt young. Her parents had encouraged her attendance at various things, her mother concerned over what she'd done, made of life, her work. As a project once she'd apparently defiled herself in certain eyes and made this public alongside a manifesto about the emptiness of moneyed heads and this complicated things. Her mother and father possessed her child because of this, and other things. Powers of attorney in so many words, the ability to say yes or no. They'd taken care of her finances and kept her fed and medicated but beyond that her freedom was limited. She attended class and spoke about her interests to undergraduates in an environment where this was safe. They saw her as threatening, she saw them as threatening. She gets up from where she was and begins to move toward her home. It won't bring happiness but she starts the process anyway. She'd slugged two breaths of wine and poured the rest atop her head toward whatever. It wasn't significant, expensive, or improving. Her fingers fidgeted against the air and she wondered at when she'd last slept. A night, years, a life. Her father's image planted on her face. The engravings then and their arithmetic. Logic as the refuse upon an unfulfilling life. Here is every reason why you're suffering and will continue to suffer. Here is medication that has proven to help. Here is potential for careers and families and loves and here is another door wherein you might enact something that veers away from all aforesaid. Hm. She wonders at the steps she takes and feels the coat around her. She'd taken it from a boy's apartment who'd played in a group utilizing electronic instruments and nothing else and they'd fucked a night when things seemed simpler. She was incapable of finishing. The boy dressed like a member of Bauhaus or Robert Smith and wore more makeup than she. Walking around his apartment stubbing her toes against books and equipment she noticed a coat and thought about the importance of the evening. Weighed against the potential importance of such an enclosing coat she decided to pick it up and leave. She'd forgotten the figure's name who might very well have fathered her kid. The coat was all left of the oaf. Arriving home she entered the bathroom and pressed her head against the mirror. A greased print was left and she pulled an old roommate's clippers from the cupboard. She'd read at times of religious women, devoted women, ritualistic women shorning their hair. She said the phrase aloud. She stood staring at herself and sunken face and pulled the clothes from her back, standing in black tights not drunk but off and turned on the machine, a waft of sobriety heaped against her sternum. She thought of women burned on stakes and pyres. She thought of cities run by women and young girls wearing constrictive footwear. She thought of balletic erosion of bodies, the image of an emaciated Renée Jeanne Falconetti against some constructed flames, shorn and beaten and finally likened to Christ. She burped wine remnants and mealy breath and kept staring at her failing. Lives had passed her by, she couldn't grab them back. She couldn't pull herself from whatever trajectory began years ago, the political, bureaucratic conversations at the university about the integrity and possibility of her work. Obscenity trials, conversations about the end of media, artwork, expression.

Step is anchored by default in the mental health of the sound according to the principles of the old. The best advice in this program: "It is working," it is facts. We harm to everyone on the list, we want to reward them. If you are unavailable to make rewards such people, so if you do not injure them completely. Other approved, the exact nature of our guilt. Do not worry about moral resolution in him, the nature of these defects is filled completely prepared Dionysian. Output think more than the force to restore our normal way of thinking and their lives. We recognize that there is strength in eating, our lives no longer swell. I want to point out, I want to retain alternative rights and rites and sacrifice various birds. We know that when he spoke to us through him efforts through prayer and medication and understanding the Lord God would present his visage. Another bad male. Nada nada nada nada nada nada nada. Nadja nadja nadja nadja nadja nadja. Who am I? Nadja, Grant me the Nadja, to Nadja the Nadja I cannot Nadja, the Nadja to Nadja the Nadja I can, and the Nadja to Nadja the Nadja. Beauty CONVULSIVE or not at all. Pierre Marie Félix Janet is here to listen.

What a boy had done was taken his father's legacy and turned it into the stuff of terror, the stuff of nightmares, a pile of rotting guts upon a legacy, a bad song for him who perished while bearded; he attended school and gained mastery in critical interpretation of certain works; he abandoned his family and left the world to rot in hell; he obsessed over the Pisan Cantos and read them front and backward eventually plagiarizing their entirety for as many local newspapers as would accept them; it was about addiction, about legacy, about leaving something behind for future generations to eat your shit and rot amid your corpses; he was a dying dog, he looked like the devil, he had no great sense of inspiration from the divine and thus when sat in rooms full of humans whining toward their god he ate his hands until they upped and left; and when they'd upped and left what he would do is suck at thumbs or chase women or break into homes for a bit of creepy crawly he was filled with such invective and steam, nothing could calm his flesh; there were lights along the roads whereon he walked, he looked and looked for a father figure in Minnesota but found none, his daddy the accomplished academic husk of a principled anvil on his mamma's guts, reciting and tyranting, letting the world warp to his needs and his desires it was enough to lose your mind and swim in seas of skin for sanity; he taught freshman English, it was nauseating, he attended NA and AA and lied through his teeth and appreciated it when citizens would leave him be because he wanted to walk and walk and once he'd walked a good distance almost Duluth to meet a woman meet her and sleep with her upon the bed within the bad hotel on her period she's on her period it chimes through his mind her cellphone rings in the morning bad news she hates the right music loves the wrong she wears a belt with a cartoon embroidered along its length he leaves and walks the street until a liquor opens up before him and he's slugging at Karkov in the aisle itself the man himself this citizen himself he's supposed to speak where he went to treatment instead he parks his car alongside the place and walks into the woods nearby removes his clothes and lays there on the grass looking up at the stars, afterward he drives throughout the place along its winds and flicks cigarettes for inmates alongside the way in plots of grass he's smiling he's always smiling he finds it tolerable if he moves he hadn't slept since he'd drunk but this was fine all was well he knew somebody from near here obsessed with methamphetamine he knew a native American fellow around here obsessed with methamphetamine he'd shown him the inside of his mouth and the jagged range of his tongue where he'd simply bitten through over time and thus his tongue looked like an inverted Mayan temple to its point and he tried to remember where this person lived and he arrived somewhere with another mate from rehab another gutless pus-eyed nutweasel and they drove together to his home smoking and smoking and smoking and smoking and when they arrived they gave each other tattoos that said various things about their addictions names of chemicals compounds and the like and then a friend unveiled some Suboxone and then another unveiled some lightbulbs and then another unveiled some methamphetamine and watching it prepared made the insides of his eyes hurt bad a girl came over they talked about their lives their struggles they talked over movies they'd seen recently and poked at their recently done tattoos and the room seemed to spin or nauseate a bit with each of their gut tendencies and come morning when the sky was heavy and nearblack they left and drove in his rustcar to a store wherein they shopped for one hour and forty-five minutes roughly staring at almost every object inside of a container containing beverages they looked and itched and purchased cheapest beer eventually and drove back to their friend's house who lived in the basement of his mother's home and she came in at nine AM to see would he go to school would Buddy go to school and they were all of them totally lost and smelling and greased with crime and thus she left and seemed depressed; the scene depressed them and thus they left and sat in a parking lot for some time smoking and smoking and smoking until they'd run clean of cigarettes and went again to store and that night they'd arranged some sort of exchange some sort of deal that would result in something altered some facial expression dragged and their entire existence made to seem a trifle against the feeling it enacted and so they these fellows the girl and the boy waited in their car and when somebody drove up and asked after their sitting they responded to eat yourself and when their friend showed up they told him this and the boy was drunk silly and flying on speed and thus he shat in snow near where their car was mumbling as the drugs were sold and when he'd finished he used corners of a case of their dirtcheap swill to wipe his hind and when he returned to the car they complained no end about his stench and so he got out was forced out of the car by them the friends the boy was forced and as he walked the street angry beyond angry he undid his buckknife from its holding and placed it in his fist opened and when he came upon a roadsign he hit the roadsign to draw brief blood and when he came upon a tree he hit the tree and blood began to shoot from fingerends and so he lay in the snow curled up having no recollection of how he'd arrived or who he might speak with and the last number he remembered beyond his left friends was the girl's and she hated his music so he called her and complained and she seemed excited at the prospect of genuine interest so off she drove to get him north of Duluth it would take some time it would take an hour maybe more and when she picked him up she drove them back to her apartment where her roommates were her anorexic roommates one of them anyway only ate yogurt from a small cup her gut was inward they watched horror films until she fell asleep and then he lay on the floor of her bedroom smoking and then she asked after his scent and then he realized his disgust and then he went into the bathroom and showered and through his clothing from the window and cared not what he would make of this tomorrow an worried not over whether he'd find clothing he went back to her room found a pair of her shorts that said bulldogs and lay back on the floor smoking menthol cigarettes smoking Salems from her pack and pacing in his mind until things died down and he fucked her with his fingers to sleep and there he fell watching television perched on her computer against his knee smoking and drinking from a bottle half water half Gatorade he fell asleep only to wake next day's afternoon depressed and smelling eggs.

Happy. I just want you to be happy. I hope for your happiness. To be happy. To feel happy. To experience happiness. To have one's life characterized as happy. One's affect. To not want. To no longer desire happiness. To have it. I am powerless. Grant me the serenity to accept the things I cannot change. Grant me the courage to change the things I can. Grant me the wisdom to know the difference. Grant me freedom from dull pains at forehead. Grant me medicine to keep the waves of depression at bay. Grant me time to watch the leaves move about. Grant me endings, sweeping tiresome endings and their story, their image, their fantasy. Grant me the ability to see through to death but not beyond. H.A.L.T. Hungry Angry Lonely Tired. I am not John Berryman. Junky. Junkie. Junke. King Junk. It's junk! Junk. Junk kit. Junk redux. The complete original text. Junky's prayer. Advice for the young. Junky's thanksgiving. Morocco. Swill. Pills. Prince of leak. Blood of Christ. Rob the Morgue. Smell the formaldehyde. Poor man's PCP. Junkies. Living death. The plague. AIDS. Father and Son addicted to heroin in Ukraine. Tulsa. Teenage lust. The ballad of Nan Goldin. Drink your cocaine. Enter voids. The spirit molecule. Pineal veer. Pet's ketamine. Darby Crash. Lexicon dribble. Somebody just get me a beer. Black triangles. They're excellent. Panic in Sharps Container. Rat—Streetwise. Flying. Yellow tops. Red tops. WMD. Like I ain't been a dopefiend all my life. I'm brown. I snorted some H. Cranberry juice. Gallons of water. Foxgloves. Digitalis. Fluoxetine. Byronic depression. Clonazepam. Methylphenidate. Sertraline. Bupropion. Seroquel. St. John's Wort. Effexor. Buspirone. Niacin. DMT. Celexa. Naproxen. I woke me from sleeping, lighting my armhair to stink. Analyzing Berryman's *Recovery*. Is it an origin story… Is it good… Is addiction literature worth piss… A conspiracy… LSD 25… Opium… The opioid crisis. A national failure. A disgrace. The War on Drugs. A performance. I hate this place and all your methods; I hate this fucking halfway house; I hate fucking recovery there is no sobriety you morons we're always on something; I don't want to go clean you idiots.

O God, my Serenity come close my God. Change me and make my Serenity O God. Courage God, Willingness God. Submission before the Godhead. Let me Change thy Will. I can. Grant my Serenity. Wisdom O God, grant it me now. Amen. Amen. Grant it me thy will. I can. Not mine, Courage. Grant me the Serenity to know. God, wisdom to accept thy changing will. Different wills and Wisdom, Courageous. Enjoying one moment at a time. That I may be reasonably HAPPY in this life. And supremely happy with Him. Amen. Trusting that He will make all things right. As it is, not as I would have it; forever in the next. Living one day at a time; taking, as He did, this sinful world courage to change the things I can; and wisdom to know the difference. Accepting hardships as the pathway to peace; if I surrender to His Will; to accept the things I cannot change; God grant me the serenity. Oh, God, my God, my quiet practice. I changed, so quiet. Oh, my God. Courage God, heaven forbid, the deity of service. Let me change will be with you. I can. Grant me the serenity. The wisdom of God, now give it to me. Amen. Amen. I admit that you desire. I can. Not my courage. Grant me the serenity to know. Lord, ah, give me courage to tell the difference I can. Give me wisdom to accept the changes you want. Will be all kinds of wisdom, courage. Enjoy moments. It may be very HAPPY in my life. HAPPY with him. I do not need it; win the future. Live from day to day; at the same time, as they did, this sinful world, courage to change the things I can; and wisdom to know the hard way difference. Accepting peace; if I surrender to his will; to accept the things I can not change, God grant me the serenity.

THREE

"*I* was a child and *She* was a child,
  In this kingdom by the sea,
But we loved with a love that was more than love—
  I and my ANNABEL LEE"
                    —"Annabel Lee," Edgar Allan Poe

You cannot engage the critical impulse alongside the other. The two eat their skins as acid. J—utilized the way furnaces utilize coal. It would enter and over time would be found a poet's happiness, an emptier notion. Nothing is working. His hands are sucked trees of no living. Dementia praecox onset wife and let me record a sea of possible scatters for the legacy. Wool. The Twin Cities. Bellowman. He would be great, of greatness. Let us slowly sip coffee and teach our students well to mop. Plomondon his favorite had working class potential. A working class boy. They'd sit on stairs at day's end as Plom held mop and talked over the state of the city, the state, the nation. He was emptied. Things were falling bit by bit from memory. Nothing held. No escape. Every appointment would slowly tear away at the heart of him. He'd sit and read of Poe or read of Melville or read of the long dead and feel comforted by their delusion. Their sense of the world as a simpler thing, and yet impossibly complicated. A gutter in Baltimore and he's out of his mind. He's Pierre, he's each of them. They are all covered in woolen cloaks and hobbling through the night drunk and mad and guiltless in the face of America's light. An ugly light. A light that persists and eats through us here in the city. It tears through my heart to see the students, their eyes as bright as death. An impossible incestuous pile of bored and boring males commiserating via secret messages and the dead. No meetings matter to me so much as those taken over by anyone other than a male. I'll listen always. The narrative ought to shift, I ought to quiet myself and publish no more work. Addicted and drunk on the work and staring. The itch in the back of Dostoevsky's brain that caused seizures and the compulsion to gamble and the compulsion to cheat and the compulsion to lie and the compulsion to write and echo outward into the ether and say something that hadn't been said and to fixate on The Body of the Christ in the Tomb. A representation of the image, the starved wrist of him and the bluing of him. The image of this echoing and passed along with letters and representations of human thought and the addict and the obsessive and the compulsive and the alcoholic the drunk and he there dragging miserable beard and wool through another door in another church to commune with the living and the dead.

As the buzzer clipped her skin she felt afraid. Her hair was long and thick, dark and perhaps her fullest feature. She slowly removed side by side every stitch until all she saw was skin and ends of stubble. She couldn't cry and so found her gut laughing. She looked at the hair piling around her feet like new roots. Nature is Satan's church. She felt the sweat on fingertips and back before looking up again and entered the shower. The water cold cleaned lengths of hair from on her ribs. It slowly warmed and she reached out to turn off the light and fell into a ball of facial expressions on the floor. The water stunk of iron and the room slowly steamed over with its film. In hospital she'd known a boy without incisors. He'd pulled one and somehow the structural integrity of his face required the other's removal. They'd meet and talk in the lounge when males and females were permitted to. They'd exchange stories about their aspirations and he told her he'd been in line to become a detective. She misunderstood him and thought he currently worked as a cop, on his way up. He corrected and said he'd studied criminal justice until he'd been found with blood pouring out of his face by concerned friends and hospitalized. He'd been inside then for months afterward, taken care of by relatives who'd rather not speak with him. She asked after his desire to police, and he corrected her again. He didn't want to walk the streets in blue. He didn't want to carry blatant firearms and mace. He hoped. He hoped to solve deaths. He hoped to take torn families and stitch them back together with his head. It wasn't about policing, he insisted. She'd never felt all too comfortable around him afterward however. She thought of scenes of the two couched just then on the floor and remembered his military hair, industrial. She ran her fingers over her skull and slapped its back. She pulled a cushiony razor from the shower's lip and ran it over her stubble until it smoothed and bled a bit. She drank the water and felt disgust. She lay back and closed her eyes in darkness and tried to ignore her limbs.

A mother dreams of son he visits for Family Week they sit and wonder sit and stare and she needs to pray and she updates him on medications, needs and they have shortcake with raspberries the campus is beautiful lush and strange, she lives amid smelling women.

You got clean it was simpler. Simpler rooms and khaki'd counselors with entire walls of accomplishment and busrides elsewhere. You've begun taking notes at meetings. You recorded a meeting once and listened to it without the consent of anyone present. You still get nauseous over this. You haven't drunk. You had a bad phase with nearbeer. You relished a likeness with Norm Pederson. Sobriety isn't grand to you, nor was drink. Drink was suicidal for you, to you, a gesture, a vying. The walls in there and carpet done up industrial and meted out days of your life reduced to schedule and video and tales of what went on. Bill W. and Dr. Bob. You read of Arthur Janov and think maybe you're exempt. You finish reading Arthur Janov years after taking it from a halfway house's shelf in Chicago after riding the train and when you get off you begin to rip up the book your copy of *The Primal Scream* and let the pages scatter around you until you find a puddle and plop the rest of the book inside the puddle. In Chicago too you read of Cocteau and *Opium* and find things a bit uninteresting as if maybe Cocteau knew a little too well that his experience on the drug could've been written about. Unsure. You watch your roommates drink after long weeks of caffeine and cigarettes and you smoke cigarettes with them and see films you see *Blue Velvet* and hear a professor offer his two cents before it plays. Your roommates do cocaine. It isn't problematic for you. You become slightly addicted to masturbating. You watch copious amounts of pornography and sit in a closet inside your room masturbating into a sock and don't feel proud of this. Occasionally you'll smoke in the room although your roommates haven't agreed for certain this is OK you figure whatever. It's there you read Johnny Cash's anecdotes about whatever and it's there you read Kay Redfield Jamison and you read letters from a drunk besotted Scott Fitzgerald to his daughter or his tormented wife and you understand some depth. You read as an addict maybe and watch television as an addict and watch films as an addict. You witness life as an addict. You enter downtown Chicago and attend classes as an addict and as an addict you walk to the Art Institute to look at their single painting by Jackson Pollock or Rene Magritte's "The Banquet" and this has a centering sensation on your gut. You attend movies frequently and try to imagine yourself as suffering along with their protagonists true or not it matters not.

"The stories are simple. A body veers off, finds comfort or quiet and at first it seems acceptable. Over time, things begin to spiral, and suddenly you're left with either the turn toward some solution, or a mountain of guilt and rationalizations just to retain the ability to keep comfort, quiet. I've formally quit drinking and using drugs twice in my life, one year apart. I quit younger than most and thus I've had constantly to grapple with this question of the heft of my addiction, back then. I didn't find myself thirty, divorced, strung out with all the earmarks of the ready-to-surrender. I was fifteen, first, and told by a perhaps too-well-versed family of interveners that I ought to quit, I seemed in bad shape. I'll tell myself stories about the end: one night I'll leave with enough money for a motel. I'll bathe for one day straight drinking in the bath and cutting away at myself. Nicks and slaps and darkness and the television out there loud as light. Standing in line for coffee I'll think on it. No longer a separation between the thoughts. To drink, take drugs. To kill myself off. They blur into the same rotgut that ups its ears at small difficulties and large maladies. Considerations slowly mutate into spiraling thoughts of shit and endings and swilling vodka hiding. I'm a hider. Somewhere in meeting rooms or offices or units awareness began to build. I drank suicidally. I took drugs not in small flights of curiosity but heaps until I'd sleep only to wake annoyed as their effects prodded my thinking and I'd be made to live. Walking down the stairs in my grandmother's home in Minnesota you'd come to a wall of portraits. These were her children, my aunts uncles and mother, mostly taken their senior years of high school toward the later 1960s so all their faces seem velvety, quaint, American.

I remember that descent of stairs better than perhaps any in my life because of each face. They've clipped themselves and jutted up at moments in my life and thus now, now that the home belongs to another family with other portraits and stories, they spread across my memory as I've needed them and they've given help, hope, perspective. Somehow through biology, through culture, through social cues and need, I've come to identify as X and Y. X being—to my mind—a loosely-bound signifier we as human animals dub 'the alcoholic.' Y being 'the addict,' yet both reduce and complicate and liken matters to such degrees as to make their value touchy. What, then, Alcoholics Anonymous? What, then, treatment? What, then, twelve steps? And yes and yes and yes, a sea. The problem and solutions of this are bound up in naming. I didn't want to clean up at first and so I went off again, 'did research' in the old timer's parlance. You hear of addiction's growth, its tendency once prodded to swell and lash back like so many wasps. You hear it and it seems odd. You hear many things seated at meetings and they seem odd, excessive, or reductive and platitudinous. Then it happens. Something happens and it clicks, the rooms call back and there you are. I remember standing in my mother's dining room. My father gruff and unconvinced, wanting military school. My mother from a line of drunks and such and thus she's in my corner, wants me back in treatment as soon as possible. I remember my mother once indicating my grandmother took great comfort in the name. She'd been intervened upon, attended treatment, experienced Family Week and my grandfather's doting, and left to stay dry and clean until her last, at some point swapping meetings for the Catholic church across their street—Elm, they lived on Elm—and it was my grandmother I first saw as a lighthouse of some otherside to the addicted state, the scrambling. Whatever preceded it, my grandmother put stake into the term, the X, the identifier that made her apart and part of, and I understand this."

The following day she woke with sticky skin, her mouth apparently dried and bitten, her teeth in pain from nightly bruxism. What she did was look around her and see the mess of an evening. She sat on the floor off the mattress a bit and looked around at walls. She grabbed a handful of crude manifestos and zines and pressed them to the center of her forehead, taking in their abjection and insight toward the times. She pulled a ripped black T-shirt over her body and fixed her tights aligned to legs. The room smelled of piss and waterlogged paper, heavy mold dragged the fixtures, outlets down. She walked to the kitchen and noted cuts along her sides. She had no idea how long she'd slept. It felt like ever. She rubbed her palmheels constantly against the sockets of her eyes until she thought she heard the bones rub. Within the kitchen she found instant coffee and turned her sink as hot as it went. The water came out steaming and she ran her fingertips beneath it watching them redden. She emptied half the container into a mug and watched it spread and smell until she caught a toxic note and grimaced at what followed. She closed her eyes and put her left hand mugless on her shaved scalp and put the cup to lips. She drank without thinking and tried not to sniff but did and it tried to retch itself back up. She forced it down and followed it all with water fresh from the sink, cold. Noted with iron she thought her eyes might slip from her head to plop in the metal. So awakened, she walked to the window and remembered waves of things, thought on her family and child, thought on her studio and artworks, thought on the work that still remained and all the feet she'd have to cross and lick before she'd arrive anywhere substantial. She detested the second, the reflection, the morning, and pressed her head to the glass of the window. People below could see her and a handful seemed to note her description. She wondered at her ugliness, what faces the students might make in sneering. She held her hand to stomach and rubbed it soft, having no way of knowing the hour passing.

FOUR

"And broken chariot-wheels. So thick bestrown,
Abject and lost, lay these, covering the flood,
Under amazement of their hideous change."
—"Paradise Lost, Book 1," John Milton

This literature becomes the new vogue and his Golden Valley is his Avalon Valley is his Stoney Lodge is his St. Elizabeth's is his Ivry-Sur-Seine is a rose is a rose. The smells in those meetingrooms was godawful. He feels the work begin to leave him. Analysis has begun and countless pictures are taken of him on his visit to Dublin, various spots in Europe. People are concerned. Had he truly thrown a woman down a flight of stairs? Had he done this? Had the muses enacted some disgusting bacchanal? He didn't care. The beard it grew. Plaguey plaguey beard. A reticence anymore at discussing literature with anyone. He prepared his cards for lectures and sweated through them until his back was soaked through and only felt at home in rooms filled with drunks and plumbers. He'd speak then as a poet then. He'd articulate things well and they seemed to appreciate his manner. He'd quote from scripture or Yeats or Coleridge on matters and compare their afflictions their innercity Midwestern afflictions to the stuff of history. He'd begun a project that would boil him down into a bit of muck, dross. Do his fellows understand him? Does his child understand him? His wife? How soon after achieving success will dementia entire set in? His life will be spent in those halls the last vestige of a dying need for spoken discourse. On entering the place he'd remembered days in Cambridge when the world seemed to coil around his whim. There were suicides then too. Emptinesses then too. A city eating itself as always. He thought over Pound then, the attempted reconciliation of the whole of history with the individual presence and the desperation to collapse a culture by way of language. He wanted none of it. He wanted a sort of remove. An abjection but made thus by its distance from commonality. He was bored. He was absolutely, terrifically bored. Every coat smelled of thorough smoke. Every room he entered harbored the same mumbles but he loved them more than university halls. The work was rejected too. Edmund Wilson a hero rejected the work from Hecate County at his remove. He understood. The work was easily marked through and erased. He'd remove things from present editions. Run through tearing it all away. And something good was given him, not from him, but given him from elsewhere. His conscience wore heavy. Life was so much misery, friends. Life, friends, is boring! Minneapolis and St. Paul were emblematic of his distemper. He'd walk hours until his shoes wore through and socks were wet trying to find something. He'd search endlessly for something. Never finding it he returned home to write and came up with halfdone work that referred endlessly to the twelve steps. It was an ordinary life. It was a bloody life. It was his failure as a poet, his poet's happiness, his endless emptiness. He wanted badly for death. He'd slither through undergraduate faces eating at his Deans' or bosses' shoes for updates, upkeep, something to continue his forward movement. The only people who seemed to care he'd done a thing at all were those in meetings, and even they had something to sell. Everywhere a memoir. Everyone a genius in those rooms, every story the darkest saddest thing you'd ever heard and every bumbling drunk who'd shit themselves at family gatherings suddenly a hero touched with divine let. Every child-leaving wife-beating scum of the earth toad pustule-tinged heap of being sitting there was limbed with light and it was light he couldn't quiet. He didn't want to. He wanted their light constantly and became addicted to its pull. The wools of his coats came close around and he'd pull them tight while smoking and mumbling about the word and its nature.

"My first sponsor on cleaning up the first time was a friend of the family. I'd called him from treatment, having spent the requisite twenty-eight days, and asked after his availability. He indicated his disenchantment with the bulk of AA proper, and though I'd only experienced a short stretch of it I thought this openness, this unwillingness to take whole hog, might do well to keep me clean. I also, those days, lied. Treatment centers in Minnesota are so widespread and various that I'd found myself in one for drunks and such under the age of twenty-four. Anytime someone came in just above that precipice they found it unsavory and moved up to Center City, Minnesota, apparently to clean up on better terms. The result was odd. The rooms were full of talkers. What we said was often in response to a mixture of legal pressure, familial pressure, and a desire to return to something approaching normalcy. We had girlfriends, boyfriends. We had lives we'd soaked in drink or mumbled through and wanted to finish school, make good on the promises of youth. I was one of them. I told stories to get myself away from there, back to friends and such who'd want to hear of what I'd seen. After days of embarrassing weeping at the phone—loud childlike whines—my parents agreed that I could return, should I meet with a sponsor and pursue strict recovery. The treatment center wanted me in Montana, for months on a sort of work-farm-recovery system that apparently worked for those in my station. I'd convinced my parents both of my dire sadness at the prospect, and the likelihood of the treatment centers being in cahoots financially, and this proved enough to get me home. That stretch of abstinence lasted around one month, and my relationship with my first sponsor dwindled into missed calls and assurances I'd been, would be, working my program assiduously. People talk about these moments. There are quotes. A common anecdote follows: while I'm in here my addiction is out in the parking lot doing pushups, on steroids, waiting for me to slip up. People talk about rock bottom, about going back out there because you're not ready to accept recovery. I don't know about the science, but the first time I used again I wound up drugged, pacing through an empty house and drinking, talking to myself and pets about the fireplace. In short order the drugs became more severe, the drink more readily available. I missed north of sixty days of school that year and on each of them I'd either sit in an elder's apartment drinking, taking lines of amphetamines or downers—whatever, whatever—or walking through the mall having purchased cheap cough syrup and Benadryl, taking the box and bottle to enact an odd, paranoiac sleepstate that must've made me a sight for all the senior citizens drifting through a shopping mall at 10 AM on a working weekday."

"On entering these spaces you're handed materials, printed literature to orient yourself to the sway and diction of a particular mode to recovery. This, hence, has made me curious. The addiction memoir, the Big Book of Alcoholics Anonymous, telling stories and conveying language and articulating as a means of what, exactly? Understanding, calm. We encounter crises, impasses in life that lead to something: for us often negative. Do this enough you become dependent on the something, the aftermath of emergency, to such an extent that the emergency dwindles in severity until finally—great taileating snake you are—your something, your X, your Y, becomes an emergency all its own. You rationalize, make explanations and write notes, send emails, texts to explain away the negative and allow yourself to live in that space of no language. To wash one's mind out in glut and spree, stand in chemical death howling barbarisms, this is the lure of the addict, perhaps. A language-free existence. A perpetual stupor needing no interior explanation and every outward qualifier is so much window dressing to keep concerned families and friends and bosses at bay. So what, then, happens in its absence? A sea of language, so ambling and smeary as to border on nonsense and thus ninety meetings in ninety days, counseling sessions and chanted platitudes, reading, writing, saying to put outside the skull what can no longer be doused or burnt." (Late meetings meant everyone was sleepy and deep in need, night is no friend to these lonely souls, some wander off and couple after, some drink coffee and wait until the last minute to drive home for television, all pace, all mumble, all whisper)

What stands out in memory are circles, their constancy, their effect in pulling words from mouths that otherwise go unsaid in life. The talking cure, a thing at once so simple that humans were bound to turn it against itself and doom it. It starts where? Vienna? Settled battlefields in Greece and conversations biding time? Its origin matters less than how we've worked it, shaped its clay to establish manifestos. Bill W. and Dr. Bob in Akron poring over lives postwar and turning rooms from simple spaces to dens of epiphany. They, however, left room for change, wanted openness and questions built into the works. Met with Carl Jung at some point to explore blurrier spiritual tie-ins and widen their acceptance.

"There is that, sure, and then the basements emanating from their spark. A man, seated, suddenly leans across a large table beneath a church to scold a room full of apparent strangers about their unwillingness to accept God into the framework. Why ask questions? Why mess with a good thing? Statistics are quoted, questions are asked and suddenly a calm is stabbed with animus. After cleaning up the second time I'd made it around ten months before losing my mind. I'd taken work as a telemarketer after testing out of high school and having no interest in college. My job was to pander for the National Rifle Association and Republican party. We were paid well for this and most who worked there seemed happy at the arrangement. I thought on it and overthought. I worried. I found myself considering pills. I found myself opening medicine chests at home and staring a bit too long at the orangey coat of plastic on my father's anxiety medicine. I couldn't sleep. Days went by and I remembered an offer for short term reacquaintance programs that existed at my parent treatment center in Center City, Minnesota. With some finagling I'd arranged a week to reinvigorate my work. I'd become addicted to reading to some degree and brought a pile of Hunter Thompson, others who'd brought me comfort. In there an old fellow told me I'd do well to watch my addictive tendency toward anything, reading included. It threw me off immensely. One night a group of us attended the meeting in the basement of the church wherein the fellow scolded our secular natures. On leaving that meeting we smoked on the steps and decided to go for ice cream. While standing in line for Dairy Queen we'd spoken about our lives, our families, what we'd do on returning home. This, oddly, brought the calm I think we'd sought within the meeting. With time, I moved away from AA proper. I saw counselors and met fellow uncomfortable souls and discussed things beyond the pale of strict recovery. I stomached artists. I looked to figures of great glut and fire like Patti Smith, William Styron, Kay Redfield Jamison. I read of Arthur Janov and Primal Therapy. I walked around neighborhoods late at night and spoke aloud with myself. I stared at the images of Robert Mapplethorpe or Nan Goldin or Larry Clark and felt a kinship with lives amiss. I read Rational Recovery and accounts on the Orange Papers or in magazines with great invective toward recovery proper. After roughly a year of devout relapse, I found myself unable to maintain as a human being the slew of lies told while drinking, using drugs. Legal complications led to a decision between time served in a small cell on a thin bed with other youths who'd made mistakes, or returning to treatment while insurance covered it and staying for the duration. Those final weeks before returning I'd occasionally use at night, in quiet, what handfuls of pills I could steal, but all told I entered rehab again in Minnesota having quit cold turkey. This was more typically the case among the age treated there: mainly turning toward it via legal discord and thus being monitored or sent to secure facilities prior to rehab. I only saw a handful of individuals strung out, but in my weeks at home a constant darkness shot through days. This might be an anomaly amid users cleaning up, I don't know. Alcoholics as a rule tend to drink severely later in life and thus longer, replacing barmates at some point with recovery groups. I'd dealt with depressive bouts longer than addictive ones, so once the drugs and drink were plucked it quickly dawned on me that large factors in my use had more to do with misery than hedonism."

Stepwork and Traditions (Eons seem to float by at Sunday meetings sat in car, there is a church, within the church there will be coffee and a meeting, coffee and a meeting, individuals sit in their cars not quite ready to walk inside, not quite separated from the lives at home to enjoy the life in there, the sun sets, it is Midwestern, there's an absence to it all, people have been sucked dry by a bit of a miserable weekend, this is their excitement—repetition—the weeks are their excitement, AA's experience weekends the way most ex-smokers experience worksites or festivals, walking by call centers or truckstops, there's an active abrasion going on between lives and resultant nausea, anger, misery, those of these lucky enough to have a bit of wealth and family are appreciated by them on particularly difficult weekends as their struggle is often palpable and easily read on face, the rest, of varying wealths, demeanors, statuses as individuals who no longer embrace their addictive personality wholly, well, there is television, there are love relationships, there are exercises, many people on cleaning up will of a sudden excel academically, able to engage humanities courses more fully as they're more comfortable with abstract prolonged paragraphs digging into the minutia of being, able to work more assiduously through other mandated courses because of their newfound love for coffee, their ability to focus for prolonged periods of time, and their interest in doing something with their lives that seems more conventionally rewarding) "I can't stand the sound of my voice clean, you know? I hear this gasping breath every time I open it at work and just can't wait for sentences to finish. I still get suicidal sometimes, y'know. I think about death too frequently maybe. My mother always used to scold us kids. *Bankrupt minds miss the ferryman.* I replay that phrase over and over now. It gets me angry again, mothers and their daughters and all, but it calms me down too. I know clean my head, my mind is anything but bankrupt. It's flooded now with occasionally fulfilling, frequently numbing thoughts. It's a botch up there. I don't know. I guess we're supposed to think on this stuff, right? Otherwise why would she say a thing like that? You always hear as much: the difference between us and the species around us is: we know we're going to die. I'm not sure that's entirely true. I mean some animals know it, but anytime I'm overly conscious of the fact of my death I'll think on my mom, and her dying, and that phrase. She wanted us to study. She wanted things to be engaging for us kids. She wanted the world to be this thing of endless possibility. It was, maybe, for a bit there. Then I found drink. I found drink and overwhelmed my head with a kind of violence. You put that stuff inside your body, you fill your body with these things you know are forms of poison. Your head is being poisoned. Your liver is being poisoned. Your heart is being poisoned. You continue, why? Because I think I was afraid to think about death. You take in poison willingly, you're engaging death. Each drink after I knew I had a problem, a bit of death. Each line, each fix, each pill, they're all potential deaths. So now I'm looking back, stuck sitting in traffic, stuck making dinner for myself and feeling dead. I'm looking back and thinking, well maybe if I'd considered death more fully, really taken my time with it, well what then?"

XXX "Violence in artwork has its place. Bataille and whatever, I dunno. I don't like interpreting things I just know when I saw those bands and saw their followers disconnects seemed to exist. My cousin saw Crass once in England in the early '80s and half the audience were National Front fascists and the other half were deadeyed anarchists with hippie leanings and the whole thing imploded into complete misery apparently. I admire the views. I admire the works published alongside manifestos you know? Long treatises about living clean, whatever. This was different, muscled. I resented that a bit. I've since heard of fascist groups in present-day Europe using Minor Threat as a sort of anthem, misunderstanding again. Straight-edge it's interesting. Now and again in meetings I see kids with massive X's on hands or Infest T-shirts and feel a bit better to know they're still around. The violence though I hold onto it. My eye it pushes at my brain."

(Persons engage in discussions mild and walk on shuffly carpet and smell the coffee and make observations, they are great and filled with hope about their futures, a young man leaves the meeting as it's getting underway and en route to the bathroom fills a small Styrofoam cup with coffee and grabs a pamphlet any pamphlet to bring along, he enters the bathroom and enters the stall and shuts the door and can now only hear muffled voices out there, he's grown sick of this place, a bit tired by all of their analysis of all the corners of their lives, and the praying, he cannot stand the praying, and the walls covered in triathlon rhetoric make him feel sick to the extent that he can't wait to leave and sit with Richard his sponsor smoking unfiltered Camels Richard's brand and feeling deep hawks of blood within his throat to under whatever'd been done to his head in there, Richard wasn't at this meeting and thus he felt fine taking his time away to shit and be at peace a bit with himself, actually he'd decided he would leave make his exit whenever he finished and if anybody mentioned it next week he'd simply say he got sick food poisoning the flu a twenty-four hour thing whatever the case may be, he was too young for this fucking place, these people had already closed their minds to almost the whole of existence, and they'd encourage him to do the same, he'd say, well why can't some things be updated? did antidepressants exist when they came up with all these rules? and they'd come back with any number of retorts carefully attuned to just that situation so that he really had no leg to stand on, it made him miserable, it made the back of his neck wince with pain and he found himself anxious to leave those places, he'd read the Orange Papers online who take the program down and humanize it a bit but even this didn't really complete a thing he just felt more bitter more frustrated more stuck, he wanted to scream at every single person in these meetings that they'd killed themselves a bit, he didn't want to force a new way of life on them but just wanted to let them know that it seemed a fragment of themselves had been killed by these rooms, the worst part was he felt sure they all felt as he felt at some point or another and whenever it came up with Richard Richard would reassure him and tell of his experience and he'd continue coming for however long, but today he couldn't handle it, today he pressed his hands against his face and yearned to reach inside his skull for quiet)

FIVE

"'Hell and shit happened, Gus. I went out cocky and never had a prayer',"

—*Recovery,* John Berryman

P—'s unwillingness to discuss himself as a sin second only to his anti-Semitism. Someone's unwillingness to solipsize being close at all to anti-Semitism would seem a huge problem with his historically-bound poetics. The anti-Semitism itself is a deplorable state that in large part should disavow the works from being considered. Yet his own appropriation of a kind of Leadbelly-inflected voice throughout is equally suspect for the time in which the work was writ. These are things that needn't bother the twentieth century. Perhaps the poet is little more than a bigot and their addictions are about as interesting as Richard Girnt Butler's sorrows. Hitler's dependence on dark chocolate. Take your pick. These are self-obsessed lives. The personal becoming the universal and all that is a crock of shit. Great works existed aside from this tendency that will never be appreciated and even the flagrance of a Céline seems more palatable than this impish racism this impish anti-Semitism this need to veil one's ineptitudes in the sheath of one's project. Everything is overrated, always. Everyone could be better, always. Every single living person could do infinitely more on a given day to ensure the comfort and stability of their fellow citizens. The Pisan Cantos and this endless obsession with the artist in turmoil, the poet in turmoil, the writer in turmoil, facing the hell of life and coming through with something transcribed, something encoded in a notebook that will be lost until it's needed. Work and work and trying to make things cohere into a usefulness thereafter. It doesn't work. It doesn't help. There is no help. There is no escaping the voice in the head and yet this compulsion to confess, to share, to give of oneself so that one's head might close itself for an hour or so, but even wanting this is the desire of the addict, even thinking this way is the pattern of the addict, the alcoholic, the drunk, the liar, his people. All his people, all his words, his opportunities, the publications, it doesn't mean anything after this. After the admission, the acknowledgement of one's state, it is finished, you are forever thereafter a part of them. The confessing becomes an addiction, the purgation. He welcomes it, confessing to his wife about every fleeting thought and writing down everything he doesn't think to say to someone's face. Slowly notebooks fill with confessions instead of work and the end result is a mass of useless writings of apology to every living thing. I'm sorry for the nature of my hurt. I'm sorry that I tore your life to shreds. I'm sorry that I made this life a torture. I'm sorry that I left you. I'm sorry, always sorry, ever and always I'm sorry. It doesn't end.

"I've said this, I know. I consumed suicidally. And yet what I'd shut my head off with were the very same things keeping AA's pamphlets printed, so returning felt apt, even tinged in light—these were my people. Everything seems minor when you've stared at it too long. I can remember early afternoon meetings in Wisconsin at Club 12 where the room had spread wide, tables lining the outskirts of a concrete floor around which chairs were filled. You sit, and you listen, and you wait. You try to think of exactly the right thing to say to set your mind aright, but once it's your turn you wind up mumbling some quick note about appreciation and smelling the roses, a lifetime's thoughts having exhausted themselves across your brow. I remember the first time I told a sponsor I'd no longer be attending meetings with them. I remember an exhilaration and a sense of freedom, a sense of owning my recovery. I remember so much driving and being alone and thinking too much thinking about my state. I remember one night returning to my treatment center, hidden. I walked up having parked far away and lay out on the lawn in darkness, knowing the place was functioning and all the newly-clean were inside sleeping, or masturbating, or hiding, or cutting themselves, or making calls and crying in offices. I took off my clothes and lay there on the grass connected, having convinced myself of something. I hadn't returned to AA after a year or more but I was sober and I was in school near to where I'd quit. I felt frantic, a mess, lost, depressed. I lay there in the dark and laughed at my idiocy and no cars passed. I'd convinced myself of my need to abstain, to be well in certain terms. I'd rejected, though, many tenets of what they'd said would keep me clean. My sponsor after treatment the second time, while living for forty-five days in a halfway house in Minnesota, was a bald fellow who worked days painting houses. I think perhaps I misunderstood the parameters he'd set between us, as I tended to call him multiple times on the house's phone with gripes large and small, assuming the flood in my thinking bore strong meaning, every morsel of thought worth interrogating until the deeds were done to death and all left were pressed-out cigarettes and sleep. I've managed to assemble a messy nine years of sobriety behind me. I worry still about its viability, its veracity if held under the scrutiny of diehard counselors and such. I occupy the mess I guess and wear it, stitching day and day together occasionally stopping to stare at their wonderments, their heaving breaths."

XXX "Another problem as I see it goes beyond whether you take drug or not. Project X becomes irrelevant when morons start dawdling into fascisms. I'd take a sea of drunk moronic fathers over one absolute Nazi. I worry over it. People turn something as simple as AA into a kind of fascism. People turn anything they like into fascism. *We fascists are the only true anarchists.* I don't know what it means. I feel oppressed in thinking about it. What a thought, a useless way to spend one's day. I carried around copies of Hubert Selby Jr. when young and now I carry around copies of the big book with notes throughout about squandered bands and lyrics. I think of someone like Bucky Wunderlich a fictional drug-addled rockstar and see the necessity for prolonged speculation about the nature of music, the nature of imbibing, the nature of drug culture itself. It's interesting. I read Myles' *Inferno* months back and found myself taking rides into the city to wander around for hours and hours. I'd come home and watch police procedurals reruns of *Homicide* or *NYPD Blue* and think about the underbelly of whatever goes on. Parents selling themselves and leaving home to slurp anthraxy coke. Children in meth-addled homes left underneath countless materials and suffocating alongside blackened bulbs as they reach death. These are forms of your children. These are forms of my children. I lived with my parents for six years in my late twenties. It felt alright. They liked that I was sober and let me stay there because of as much and I'd littered my walls with posters again and started bands and seen bands and joined up with various likeminded people who were young and forced either to quit or die. I read about Dave Insurgent and felt grave pain. His girlfriend murdered by a serial killer and both of them already besotten with dope and misery. Living like Alexander Trocchi and co. but in the early '90s when the War on Drugs took hold. She falling to the murderous idiocy of Joel Rifkin—another glut—and he falling in turn. Swelled up with dope it thickens blood until a person's face seems droopy with opioids. Receptors in his brain slowly dwindling over years of use and Sid Vicious hacking up his guts in someone's gaff and Nancy Spungen holding his head against her leathers swilling booze in her parents' home asking for money asking for money asking for money these are not people with whom you discuss the nature of printed texts, of living, of political discourse or the violence apparent in average runofthemill society. Joyce didn't take years writing *Finnegans Wake* he took years drinking himself into a stupor over the mess of Lucia of Nora of Samuel everyone hounding his head and pulling him down the world pulling him down expectation making him swell or swelter or shock himself into stupors that could only be left when absolutely piss besotten drunk. He'd walk with Hemingway and when picked on Hemingway would fight in his defense because Hemingway was an inept moronic oaf filled up with self-loathing for some anormative yearn only in texts that went to print after he sucked good gun."

People are scum. Hurt people hurt people. Self-mythology. Struggles take on the stuff of history. Histories take on the earmarks of struggle. Become whipped. Become martyred. Become beplagued spectacles and addiction only makes it worse, alcoholism only gives it shape, a name, a place in society that can in turn offer some narrative of redemption. Life is a kind of scum. Scum around a drain. Existence is by its very nature parasitic, and even typing his works he can't hold fast to this Cioran vein. Their selfishness makes him nauseated and yet he can embrace its utility. The lines not written in a kind of pirated aping are palatable and sometimes moving. It makes you wonder at the heights of genius, is all. These apparent deviants only offerings extremes of the culture they're purporting to reject. Pound worse for Pound's indecipherability. A maze and the key is buried in a select body of work that also resulted in a demeanor that embraced whole hog fascism and the rejection of a race of humans. One would do well to wonder. Everything is political even the old chestnut. One would in turn rather have the arrested, bloated, irascible body of D.A.F. Sade than these hidden, suffering bodies. Perhaps this is the difference. A loss of energy. One continues forth in all its squalor making moments, the other leaves a trail of apologia to continue slightly unreadable in their determination to be hailed as Genius, Significant, Strugglers. Outside I am powerless. Outside I need help. Outside I give up. Outside I ask the void. Outside I am wrong. Outside I shout it out, my wrongdoing. Outside I keep myself in check. Outside I walk the earth. Outside I apologize, always apologizing. Outside I ask for light, lightness. Outside I admit dark, darkness. Outside, tired, I persist. We lived well in there, perhaps too well I GIVE UP I need help I ask the void I am wrong I shout it out, my wrongdoing I keep myself in check I walk the earth I ask for light, lightness I apologize, always apologizing I admit dark, darkness tired, I persist.

GIVE ME A LITERARY CULTURE STEEPED IN BLOOD AND PISS AND SHIT AND OWNING THAT. GIVE ME PASOLINI GIVE ME TROCCHI GIVE ME GUYOTAT GIVE ME SADE GIVE ME GENET GIVE ME BATAILLE GIVE ME GIVE ME DWORKIN GIVE ME MARECHERA GIVE ME ACKER GIVE ME SQUALOR GIVE ME THE VILE STATE OF THE HUMAN PIG AND LET ME REVEL IN IT DO NOT QUALIFY DO NOT GIVE MATTERS CONTEXT TEACH ME HOW AND WHY THESE THOUGHTS EXIST AND LET ME LOSE MYSELF BENEATH THAT TEXT.

XXX "Sleep comforts me now. I still go through the motions of being but any semblance of a scene is gone. I encountered many many people with smiling heads full of potential ready to offer me things that might save me from myself. I listened. I appreciated every step. I left for China once when I'd saved money and spent my days wandering around trainstations drinking from vending machines wearing the clothing I'd stolen from various exes that then made up my wardrobe I slept in fields occasionally on the foothills of larger ranges of mountain I saw bamboo growing naturally it wasn't exceptional I just enjoyed what was offered you understand what was given."

Affirmation of the necessity of ritual in the lived days of a human animal in the twenty-first century. You sobered up young which became touchy, issuesome. You went to rehab once for a month at fifteen, then relapsed and returned next year to turn seventeen while admitted and remain under someone's care for six months thereafter. You started to drink and use whatever at hand when eleven years old, and although the short span between then and abstinence was thus, your tendency proved it a sufficient jaunt to warrant cleaning up. An answer does not exist. Often you'll feel haunted. Occasionally you've slipped back into those rooms to dawdle a bit and listen mostly. Henry, Henry. It helps affirm, but nothing quite like the clear day, nor the besotted televisual mind. Watch something, Henry. Become numbed, sure, but hope. You read an emptiness in most addiction literature as one reads emptiness into most literature content with a certain understanding of subjective human experience. Nothing seems more apt in this respect, an addiction to insomnia perhaps, an obsession, a monomania. All you have is a sea of referents and texts, stitched together with observation and image, phrase and sentence. An underrated work of addiction literature perhaps being Cocteau's *Opium*. You'd written it off initially for its minor nature, but looking back its loose structure and diary's reach seems larger. The single-line drawings of Cocteau dense with meaning for the emptied gutless dog. It is never as if there's one clean answer, and this poses every problem you as sufferer have had. What you mean to express is inexpressible, unfortunately, except perhaps via the means of the fictive, the slippery interplay of text and reality. Therein you've found some solace, and though not everyone buries themselves in types of texts to achieve some comfort, the process of ritualizing and re-ritualizing lives becomes constant. You stare at Gass' statement that he writes because he *hates. A lot. Hard.* and find your comforts. Military-minded citizens fold bedsheets up to meet some standard. Cook and play your Dean Martin, your Emerson audiobook, whathaveyou. The problem inevitably congeals its way into some new pursuit, and there you find yourself.

Much ado exists wondering just where the line exists between "addict" or "alcoholic" or "normal drug user" or "everyday drinker" so where you could you've attempted to keep matters simple to find sense. To wit, the depressive—and herein exist further complications, madnesses (Henry, Henry), but the serotonin/dopamine deficiency model resulting in low moods/energy, suicidal ideation, and a spectrum of emotional despondency might suffice—is like any human animal. The depressive seeks out ritual. The "normal" person seeks out ritual. The depressive's ritual might tend more toward destruction, and the "normal" person's more toward construction. There are no absolutes, unfortunately, but as you've observed them "addicts" and "alcoholics" tend at least to carry aspects of the depressive, and hence develop killing rituals to carve out some meaning in life that in turn overwhelm. The quasi-functioning human animal does the same thing, and this can lead to "negative" results in turn. People become addicted to any range of things for any range of reasons. Your search and writing thus has less to do with attempting to identify the True Addictive Personality as with expressing your own contempt and efforts to abstain after addiction became realized. This is not to say they have no place. The life of the drunk is often long and winding, and thus on sobering up a total replacement of friendships, and behaviors must take place. There the mode makes sense. Elsewhere, however, or in the case of someone simultaneously bogged by depression and stupor, an alternative glance might prove helpful. Think of Poe, of Bobby Liebling of Burroughs of Byron of massive emptinesses. They were vying. They were reaching toward some imperceptible speck, a void beneath. It is boredom.

It is that. You gutless dogs are bored to retching. What of it? More vying, emptiness. You drank and took pills as a ritualistic gesture that aligned with your gut instinct that being alive was overrated. A toast to disinterest, to fear, to anger, to contempt, to death. In meetings on quitting you'd realized you'd have taken anything, on any occasion, so as to obscure what was. You once snuck into your neighbor's home and took a handful of random pills, swallowing all and spending an evening pacing around your mother's basement swilling.

I WANT TO KILL MYSELF. I WANT TO KILL MYSELF. I WANT TO WATCH MY SON BECOME BORN. I WANT TO WATCH MY DAUGHTER BECOME BORN. I WANT TO WATCH MY GRANDSON SWING. I WANT TO WATCH MY GRANDDAUGHTER DANCE. I WANT TO SLEEP IN AA MEETINGS. I WANT TO SLEEP IN HIGH SCHOOLS. I WANT TO SLEEP IN REFUSE. I WANT TO WAIT FOR GOD. I WANT TO PRAY WITH YOU EMPTY. I WANT TO STAND IN NIGHT CLUBS. I WANT TO BE A FAMOUS CORPSE. I WANT TO BE MADAME TUSSAUD. I WANT TO EAT WAX. I WANT TO SMELL DEATH. I WANT TO SPEAK AT CONFERENCES FOR MONEY. I WANT TO EAT WAVES OF MONEY. I WANT TO BECOME PREGNANT. I WANT TO BECOME DEATH. I WANT TO INVENT NARCOTICS. I WANT TO INVENT PLAGUES. I WANT TO WATCH THE PLACE FALL APART. I WANT TO SEE YOU THERE. I WANT TO FEEL BETTER. I WANT TO FEEL ALIVE. I WANT TO FEEL DEATH. I WANT TO EAT MY WORDS. I WANT TO DRINK. I WANT TO WATCH MYSELF DRINKING. I WANT TO INHALE CHEMICALS. I WANT TO TURN MY MIND OFF. I WANT TO BECOME ASSASSINATED.

SIX

"The decomposition of the sugar is therefore due to a condition of instability transferred to it from the unstable andchanging ferment, and only continues so long as the decomposition of the ferment proceeds,"
 —*Alcoholic Fermentation*, Arthur Harden, Ph.D, D.Sc, F.R.S

Look at the way he's cultivated space. There's an outwardness to poets, maybe. Inside there's an assumption of bereft gut and bones and so much smoke, out there's frailty and just beyond the skin a singing that lets him feel alive and alright on earth. He smoked almost constantly, smearing ash against a sea of modern works of poetry and dissertations, prose and theses, countless things for his review. Papers on any number of subjects all somehow tied to the lectures he'd strung together, some even featuring notes concerned at his state, wondering if he truly felt O.K. He truly felt O.K., little else. He did enjoy the groups, the meetings, but even they wore on a bit and lost their height. He became stuck pondering imagery after life. He became stuck in Irish mores. What, Beckett. What, Molloy. What, Godot. Walls of galleys lined his front hall and he pulled from them at random occasionally picking up interesting bits. A poetry collection dedicated to the journal *Merlin* and made of debauched nods to various personae therein. A new study about the occult and Pound. Reinterpretations of the Pisan Cantos. He became lost in thought a bit then. His lineage undeniably bound to His. He thought of the brawny chest in pictures seemingly having ripped through shirt and whitened hair and always that aquiline goatee constantly villainous, tyrannical. He wondered about the caked dirt upon his skin while jailed in Italy. The fascist tracts that bled out there. An addict, perhaps? A neurotic? Schizophrenia? Time won't offer these answers. The extreme of any art might very well be addiction. Pound embodied this. It is impossible to continue under the strain of history without making certain choices. These choices left some mad. These choices left some dead drunk or merely dead. These choices tore away at the self of Scott Fitzgerald and Zelda Fitzgerald and their determination to remain there for one another even through the torrid hell of it seems more important than any line Hemingway wrote. The world is enacting a process against us, attempting to remove the child within or the thought within of possibility and freedom. The will is fermented. The body is fermented. There is nothing left to read, to record, we have only to persist and transcribe the cracks.

If the gods be a danger to Alcoholics change your behaviors. Inventory and other personal injury, I want you to lean on me. With a sense of same in regard to the acts you bring to life, after you have conquered. Make a list of all damaged and further damage all. Generous strength training. The acts of a problem in Satan, they confess, not without reason do we adopt, destructively, these principles, our Generous Power of Truth. To do judgment to god, you and your care, not that you wish to understand. By what constant temptation weak soul bends to drink the exercise of the stay. Several times you have become friends with others, as many as all of your forever, the members Errol Flynn—if he does not want to turn the good of his friend to drink, argue otherwise. Leadership their struggle and importance of the Godhead, from the facts and to take their drinks from the wells of the Cure. Hath he removed our research and fearless inventory. You'll try not to turn to the awakening of the spiritual life of the Church after the other, the grave. The opinions of peons, occult atheists. Now concerning our gifts they are ever. Pray to God and do not indulge in immoral flagellation and dance soulless around the flames consulting the heavens in passivity. Conduct investigations into the lives of your peers and report, Generous Power Honor. We have the victim refused. For the fact that you want to, do not want to be a victim.

"Once when I was whenever I read something in a magazine about a guy who took these pretty harmless pills so he could stay clean maybe like Chantix now for smoking I dunno he stayed clean though after trying rehab trying AA trying NA trying CA trying GA trying Al-Anon when his (second) wife drank as much as he did and he convinced himself it was her fault. He was an asshole maybe but he took this stuff in Europe I think and there where he took it he suddenly saw things align and he seemed to get better. Maybe like that guy in Rational Recovery I can't remember the particulars but he seemed to tap into something and the first thing he needed to do was tell everybody about this grand conversion experience. Maybe that's the problem. Maybe when you encourage somebody to tell their own story they become a little obsessed with its particulars. Everyone in AA is a storyteller (liar) maybe. Everyone everywhere is a storyteller (liar) at some point or other I guess but this guy seemed so convincing. The sober memoirist. I've suffered. Come join me in this and watch my debauched trek through hell to find paradise in a room full of plastic chairs and adults weeping over their status while their families fall apart. Maybe I'm too cynical. Is there something to the poet that makes him or her so thick with refuse? Lying? Berryman was simultaneously one of the great geniuses America's produced and one of the most obnoxious frauds. P.T. Barnum. We do not live in a world where solutions simply exist as solutions. We live in a world where solutions immediately become currency. Everything and everything becomes exploited. Everything turns to shit eventually. Even Bill with his Johnny Horton presence admitted to his ineptitude while establishing the whole mess, his curiosity about LSD. But then death, and we as citizens of the earth on which Christ once walked are unable to cope with someone who imparted decent advice then dies. They become a martyr whether we call them this or want it so. It becomes problematic sure. Everything becomes problematic. People fighting and ruining their lives over this every day. It is a life-ruining thing. There's nothing much to think about. There's entirely too much to think about. We all become addicted to coffee but this is nothing. Balzac drank fifty cups a day and we are certainly not Balzac, none of us. Then the celebrities. Pieces of entertainment that convey the message of a given organization. A sad male pornography addict. Blah blah blah. We are self-supporting. No we aren't. We have the earmarks of a cult or religion but we are not this. I don't know. This guy seemed fedup with AA and NA like I said so he goes and starts taking these pills and I'm sure if I'd looked I could've found funding to his message from Pfizer. It's all so pathetic. Snake oil. We will unite in our discouragement toward uniting in any formal capacity. In a way it's preying too, that's what's sad. It ought to be researched. I read again that ADD/ADHD are the two most researched diagnoses regarding mental health of late. It depressed me. I'm like, wait. Wait. Explain this to me. Half the rhetoric I see about those afflictions has to do with their less than stable acceptance in society. Kids taking speed. Seven-year-old depressive prescribed speed when acting off only to lose appetite and interest further and wind up hospitalized. It's me, it's me. It's maybe pathetic. Maybe it's that. What about depression? Is it legitimate? Dürer and Byron and van Gogh and Lincoln all taking concoctions trying to treat something they felt but what if they were just bored? What if they just needed a better diet and exercise and they'd convinced themselves it couldn't just be that because of how special they seemed to everyone around them? All are special. But all can be special in their dull ways. I rather like that. I always loved janitors. My favorite thing about Henry Darger isn't that he created all this art, but that he did so in his off-hours while working as a janitor. His work is only great when weighed against the dull nature of everything else, but removed from the dull nature of everything else his work becomes obnoxious and moneyed. Henry Darger goes to Art School. Henry Darger lectures at Yale about the confluence of religious mania and childlike wonder in his work, his stories, his mythos. Let's not assume either that he was heroic for not being famous or something. Let's assume his work was rejected by stuffed shirts the world over and maybe this makes it better. I'm unsure. This fellow who took the pills he had all these scenes walking around interesting locations lost in thought and running toward drink, chainsmoking neglecting his family every such thing until he finally found the perfect thing for him. I wonder at that. I wonder at exemption. The problem might be our tendency to mythologize the fragments of our lives. The problem might be the encouragement for everyone to tell their stories and make them stab. It's an ugly world, everywhere. Perhaps those places that don't have a word for suicide never existed. Utopia isn't a problem because it only exists in the abstract. Those dancing figures around a massive Olympian track in *Metropolis*. Our lives have to be more than working eating walking around bearing children and communicating. This is the problem, our inability to sit in a chair in a room and occupy our thoughts. The problem is." (He writes this over three sessions and sends it to the group email of his area's AA listings, his desktop is lousy with half-measures, a picture of Raymond Federman in makeup, he won't receive a response to his email but after he masturbates [blah blah blah] and it feels as good as a meeting, he sleeps)

The addict and the everpresent question of death, the notion that we're all working toward that one goal. You've been sifting through materials allover trying to find likenesses. You find sleeping. You find fathers. You find mothers. You find a world bogged down by alcoholisms that push lives to great disarray; and make sense. You wanted an answer. You wanted to make something worthwhile from all that dreck. What you found instead was further language.

What Henry became obsessed with was language. The besotten Joyce maybe or the notion of Dublin torn to guts and drunkt dead as the light faded June sixteenth. The night. Finnegans night. Fine again. Finn, again. Fin, again. Finnegans, wake! Finnegan's wake. HCEARWICKER. He became convinced the tune the old man hummed who drove them was about Molly Bloom. Stories of a couple broke and hopeless along the Liffy. *Charlie's on the dole and they sleep in strawberry beds.* He sang it and took them to the YMCA for them to sit in lockerrooms feeling normal again feeling alive not dead new life breathed into them carrying them over across something across the river two coins in their eyes awakened sobriety medallions placed over their eyes on dying maybe perhaps not. A god of the dead and Charon. He became obsessed with names noted them laid them down on scraps of paper until his pockets were full like Molloy sucking stones he'd read them over lying in bed with a small lamp then read bad thrillers he enjoyed the rides most leaving treatment leaving rehab feeling free writing scraps singing songs listening to the old man hum in his thick Irish seep on air and everyone speaking behind him talking about drugs talking about girlfriends talking about competitions talking about drink talking about smoking talking about the nature of addiction obsession mania perhaps. I am not a sex addict. I am not an alcoholic. I am not an addict. I am a nymphomaniac. I am a drunk. I am a dopefiend. He enjoyed their talking but needed to leave he felt he needed to flee this place and head someplace else it made him think on dying he never much thought about death about the end of his life except in the abstract or in a brief teenage urge toward sleep he'd feel it maybe overwhelming then. Henry would leave and become addicted to gambling picking up lottery tickets smoking compulsively constantly playing things on his computer for money trying to come up with schemes for more creating music his eyes were sunken in he'd relapse frequently then pick up more lottery tickets resented the meetings resented the rooms the lives inside them he was drinking himself to death inside of rooms alongside you you drank and sat there spitting on yourselves listening to contemporary music trying to die a bit eke a bit more toward death to feel complete he wanted it worshiped it and walls only proved a step toward oblivion he'd have it. It was great. He'd won money. He was successful because he bet with a multitude of groups around the city and made more and more money and felt alright about himself his life but nothing seemed to quite click for him like drinking he'd bring home bottles of whiskey something to turn his brain off he'd say something to start the weekend a bit and suddenly he'd be dead drunk outside your place down on the street listening to the neighbors watching as people walked out toward violence a metropolitan way you lived down the street from where you got your haircuts and there you'd spend hours sobering up next day with light in your eyes receiving cuts and it could take a whole day and you'd eat a large piece of bread apiece and feel much more at ease having soaked the swill within and you'd both shower and laugh at eachother and spit and vomit up blood and smoke in there and your lives together were kind of seamless kind of nice you both wanted to make art and you both hated absolutely everyone outside of the apartment so you might stay close not fucking but something feeling there for one another like brothers maybe you'd imbibe the same things and suffer the same. You told him when you died you'd like to hang yourself it might feel right you know wrap a thick cord around your neck then step off sort of oldfashioned it might feel just right. He said he wanted to die by taking a substantial overdose of heroin and you understood this but made him expand on it he said it would be the best feeling in your life followed by absolute emptiness and that's all he'd ever really worked toward you think that ultimate quiet you wanted to sleep and feel at ease. You respected him for this and listened as he told you and you'd watch old '70s pornography with rooms full of sweat and bad speaking and things were calm.

TV WUNDERKAMMERN (after Kenneth Anger) - "ALYSONN & TYLER – CRACK COCAINE, MORPHINE/CODEINE" . . . "GALE AND TINA – GAMBLING/SHOPPING" . . . "PAMELA & TOMMY – PRESCRIPTIONS/SELF-MUTILATION" . . . "ALESSA & BREANE – GAMBLING/CRYSTAL METH" . . . "SARAH – CRYSTAL METH" . . . "TRAVVIS & MATTY – CRYSTAL METH/CRACK COCAINE" . . . "PETE & REN – VIDEO GAMES/ANOREXIA NERVOSA" . . . "CINNATUS – PRESCRIPTIONS" . . . "CRISTIAN & KELLEY – ALCOHOLISM/EATING MATTERS" . . . "KEN AND MAERK – DRINK/PRESCRIPTIONS" . . . "HUNTER & RALPH – FIREARMS/MEDICINE CHEST" . . . "JOHNNY – MIRRORS/HIS SMELLS" . . . "EDIE – AMPHETAMINES/ART" . . . "ELVIS – STOMACH/AMERICAS" . . . "FARLEY – CHICAGO/LAPSED CATHOLICISM" . . . "RUSSELL TYRONE JONES – OPPOSITION/SPECTACLE/COCAINE/CHILD-REARING/VIOLENCE" . . . "BELA – MORPHINE/OLD HOLLYWOOD/ABJECT DARKNESS" . . . "DIANE ARBUS – BARBITURATES/WRISTS" . . . "LESTER BANGS – DARVON/VALIUM/NYQUIL" . . . "BIG MOE – CODEINE" . . . "LENNY BRUCE – MORPHINE" . . . "DARBY CRASH – DARBY CRASH" . . . "DJ SCREW – CODEINE/GENIUS" . . . "SIGMUND FREUD – DR." . . . "IRA HAYES – DRANK HIMSELF TO DEATH/EXPOSURE TO THE ELEMENTS" . . . "WHITNEY HOUSTON – ACCIDENTAL DROWNING/AMERICA" . . . "MALCOLM LOWRY – ALCOHOL/BARBITURATES" "BILLY MAYS – COCAINE/

HEART" . . . "KEITH MOON – DOSTOEVSKY" "PRINCE – GENIUS" . . . "PIMP C – SLEEP" . . . "POE – LAUDANUM/DT's" . . . "BRAD RENFRO – CALIFORNIA' . . . "BON SCOTT – ROCK 'N' ROLL" . . . "DASH SNOW – BAUDELAIRE" . . . "JOAN VOLLMER, JOAN VOLLMER, JOAN VOLLMER, JOAN VOLLMER, JOAN VOLLMER, JOAN VOLLMER, JOAN VOLLMER, JOAN VOLLMER, JOAN VOLLMER, JOAN VOLLMER, JOAN VOLLMER, JOAN VOLLMER, JOAN VOLLMER, JOAN VOLLMER"

SEVEN

"The drunken ship is fast filling with water. Not a man at the pumps, not an arm at the helm. Having destroyed their friends, the crew fall upon each other. Close under their bow rave the breakers of a rocky shore, but they hear it not. At intervals they seem to realize their condition, and their power even yet to save themselves, but they make no effort. Gloom, and storm, and foam shut them up against hell with many thunders,"
—*Alcohol and the Human Brain*, Rev. Joseph Cook

A life is an awareness a consciousness of certain matters of breathing of hunger of desire perhaps desiring machines he'd considered this and thought endlessly in theoretical terms about his poetics and how it fits within a larger canon the work seems to fall to bits but he's sticking with it due to something some drive and this might be the French desire the May 1968 desire he's uncertain but keeps pressing on. There is a push, something guiding him perhaps or at least propelling and when he swills and when he drinks and when he squalors and when he writes it's all the same he leaves a mess. Somewhere, he vomits himself upon something some page and it becomes a work of something abstraction expressionism he wallows in his own filth and organizes it into poetic works. He wallows in absolute stasis in uncertainty in near-death and it's only here he seems to find his happiness that starved starving state of near-unconsciousness that takes him far and far from life. He wants to live there he'd like to live there buried there where nobody touches him or wants to he'd like the courage to place the cold of a gun against his temple he'd like the courage to swallow his wife's medication he'd like the courage to slit his wrists within the tub perhaps he'll read first something good something excellent a review a piece of newsprint something that touches the living just one last time before he ends it all. He'd love to end it all see what death feels like deep within its clutches a nice sentiment a great notion he's pressing for it vying toward it and all he feels is tired. All he wants is sleep he wonders did his mother have it did his father have it this desire this yearn this tendency to move and eat what came and throughout Minneapolis throughout Minnesota throughout the Midwest and campuses everywhere there seems to be this leap to death this tendency to want the world to fall apart and this feels nice like the clutch of a warm wool sweater against the radiator sitting there some morning sick with aftermath and children weeping and his wife dissatisfied and his life a selfish trap of nonbeing he'd like to end it take the pills cut the wrists intake the bullet and simply let things stop but something will not let him it makes him sick it's impossible to stomach he wants to go to treatment again he wants to be hospitalized again only in there did it make sense where is his St. E's he wants to bury his head beneath the floor in his St. E's and welcome the inanity of not cohering with reality with their reality he wants to assist Whitman during the War he wants to transcribe for Chaucer he wants to lend his life some meaning in service of their poetics and all for naught he sniffs the air before his face and wonders at his body on the bed in St. E's weeping there clutching his sheet there sweating through everything muttering about Li Po and the rivers muttering about Joyce and the rivers wondering about the storm he visits his withering bare chest pressed against the light and nurses they both drink coffee he asks after progress everything has become political and steeped in bureaucracy and he finds himself yearning for the comforts of the old campus there is something in his demeanor that makes him feel as though a plagiarist as if his entire modus operandi had been lifted from his living but then he thinks over the mistakes he thinks over the years he thinks over the work written and the radio broadcasts and something lessens something starts to feel O.K. and he notes that he won't likely leave but there is something foundational in his state of course D.A.F. Sade chimes in at witnessing his gut but this seems new this seems different his status isn't quite like the status of those old artists he is living in the modern world he is compulsive he is obsessive he is monomaniacal and his affectation is apparently derived from the state of modern things not unlike the emanating tendency of the *Cantos* the outward glance always always sampling from history always taking always giving always appropriating and rendering new and (blah) it makes him shake a bit with something foreign some leaving of the past behind his hospitalization paves the way for something his madness paves the way for something for the hulking state of the WRITER the ARTIST the GENIUS in the twentieth century and it becomes terrifying again as he remembers his missteps and he too yearns for Europe he too yearns for something older the simplicity of D.A.F. Sade's desired grave perhaps the acorns they've stuck inside his skull and taken growth there. When he leaps from the bridge it is as from a window, and he takes with him the home of every drunk living, and later years later in 1995 later the Frenchman will leap in turn and fall and they will both fall in perpetuity fall toward the earth.

You entered rooms and saw people seated in circles discussing things and somehow pulled from this their ends, beginnings. They'd discuss family, friends, lovers they'd lost. There was a great emptying in confronting death, life, so publicly. They harbored no substantial hopes about what the life might become beyond this. All their dreaming sort of left with numerous arrests, perhaps. People changed their appearances frequently. People came to meetings just from the gym and looked alright. You'd look at them and think being alive is alright. And then you'd remember the book of abjection in which you'd read that. These people were filled with a kind of love. These people had each other over whenever possible to maintain something like a normal social life. You enjoyed their company, and yet winced a bit whenever things took too exacting a shape. Once you hid spits you'd done on the floor of the place in the back where nobody could see. Once you'd fucked males and females from multiple groups within a given year and things became quite hectic, you entered your mother's room broke on Mother's day morning asking after money to buy the pill. You were mutually sober and a bit fucked and maybe that made it alright. Once you'd spent weeks on end obsessing over movies in the next city and seen as many as you could. Derek Jarman's films played once for two weeks straight and you watched them thinking over emaciated bodies done in by death. A jubilee. My love is like a red red rose. Once you'd dreamt of attending writing workshops in a city where things were violent. You read Christopher Coe and felt you'd connected with something transcendent about being a person. You read Tim Dlugos and felt same, a spirituality not bogged down by any language. You read Hervé Guibert, and read of Hervé Guibert, and felt connected with a vulnerable humanity. You wanted more vulnerability in your days. Your sobriety seemed to depend upon it. If you were open, and vulnerable, and capable of being hurt by the world, well that was O.K., wasn't it? Once a professor had told you how he worshiped *Apocalypse Now* and you watched the film *Hearts of Darkness* made by same director's wife and at one point your professor discussed director as a sensitive artist and this felt real, this felt genuine. You still play over those scenes of him sitting there filled with coffee having lost weight discussing Irwin Allen and asshole college professors and pretentiousness and the moment when you finally say *fuck it*, that all you know is that you're going to witness this art; and in turn you want it to have answers, and not just on the surface but on countless levels. He says this and you still play it over in your head. He says this and you feel you've tapped into the why of something needing to be created, something asking after its creation. He says this and you bow your head and let yourself become sweaty and walk way out beyond any point in the city that you recognize until your thoughts race and you're terrified and paranoiac and coffee is eating away at your guts and your partner's back home and your child's back home and you need to return to them soon enough but you want one more minute, one more step into some kind of beyond or unknowing that makes all the monotony worth it. Every stitch of civilization suddenly becomes inconvenient toward your ends so you continue walking, picking up trash and feeling it within your palms sweat and get pulled in wind and your eyes are leaking and your forehead's leaking and it hurts it's filled with salt and you continue on until you feel as if your legs are going to split apart you continue on living and worship a kind of death you step way out and feel your heart collapse against the splendor of what's before you and suddenly you stop and kneel and rub your face deep into the rock and mud and scream and weep and tell yourself that all will be alright, that endings and graves and bills and loans and banks and families and dinners and breakfasts and films and books and televisions and poems and standups and games and walks and runs and rides and highs and pulls and meetings and meetings and meetings and sponsors and sponsees and steps and worries and anxieties and fears and mothers and fathers and fences and knives and tears and plastics and coffees and smells and noises and towns and vistas and diners and opportunities and actors and interventions and relapses and chemicals and pills and sisters and wives and brothers and friends and chairs and rooms and walls and hospitals and schools and pages of work are all of what will pull you, all of what will gauze your brain. Come away.